JANE AUSTEN IN AND OUT OF CONTEXT

JANE AUSTEN IN AND OUT OF CONTEXT

Shinobu Minma

KEIO UNIVERSITY PRESS

JANE AUSTEN IN AND OUT OF CONTEXT

Published by Keio University Press Inc.
19-30, 2-chome, Mita, Minato-ku
Tokyo 108-8346, Japan
Copyright © 2012 by Shinobu Minma
All rights reserved.

No part of this book may be reproduced in
any manner without the written consent of
the publisher, except in the case of brief
excerpts in critical articles and reviews.

Printed in Japan.

ISBN978-4-7664-1961-0

First edition, 2012

Contents

Acknowledgements vii
References to Jane Austen's Works ix

Introduction 1

CHAPTER 1 General Tilney and Tyranny: *Northanger Abbey* 13

CHAPTER 2 Marianne and Mary: *Sense and Sensibility* 31

CHAPTER 3 Too Much Antipathy towards Too Much Formality: *Pride and Prejudice* 49

CHAPTER 4 The Other Side of an Orderly World: *Mansfield Park* 71

CHAPTER 5 Self-Deception and Superiority Complex: *Emma* 91

CHAPTER 6 An Organization that Works: *Persuasion* 111

Notes 133
Bibliography 149
Index 157

Acknowledgements

This book has grown very slowly—over some twenty-five years—and early versions of the arguments advanced here appeared in several journals during that period. Chapter 1 and 5 were originally published in somewhat different form in *Eighteenth-Century Fiction* as 'General Tilney and Tyranny: *Northanger Abbey*' (Vol. 8, No. 4, 1996) and 'Self-Deception and Superiority Complex: Derangement of Hierarchy in Jane Austen's *Emma*' (Vol. 14, No. 1, 2001). Chapter 2 and 4 first appeared in *Studies in English Literature* (The English Literary Society of Japan) as 'Marianne, Mary, and Jane Austen: A View of *Sense and Sensibility*' (Vol. 68, No. 2, 1992) and '*Mansfield Park* and English Society in the Early Nineteenth Century' (English Number, 1990), the latter of which has undergone considerable revision. A much earlier—and very different—version of Chapter 3 appeared in *Journal of Arts and Letters* (The Keio Society of Arts and Letters) as 'Too Much Antipathy towards Too Much Formality: Jane Austen's Social Criticism in *Pride and Prejudice*' (No. 50, 1986). A portion of 'Introduction' also appeared in the same journal as 'Propriety and Hierarchy in Jane Austen's Novels' (No. 73, 1997). Chapter 6 was originally published in slightly different form in *The Journal of the Jane Austen Society of Japan* (No. 5, 2011) as 'An Organization That Works: The Gentry and the Navy in *Persuasion*'. I should like to express my appreciation to the editors of these journals for permission to use the material. My thanks are also due to each journal's anonymous readers for their helpful comments on earlier versions of the material. I am also grateful to my old friends from my graduate school days at Keio University, who offered valuable criticisms and suggestions in the early stages of this study, and who have kept encouraging me to this day. Finally I should like to express my deepest gratitude to the memory of my teachers, Masao Kaiho, Shinsuke Ando, and Kei Koike; without their inspiring guidance this book would not have come into being.

References to Jane Austen's Works

References to Jane Austen's works are to the following editions:

The Novels of Jane Austen, ed. R. W. Chapman, 5 vols., 3rd edition (London: Oxford University Press, 1932–34); reprinted with revisions 1965–69.
Jane Austen's Letters, collected and edited by Deirdre Le Faye, 3rd edition (Oxford: Oxford University Press, 1995).

The title of the novel (indicated by its initial letters) is cited in the text only when the reference would otherwise be unclear.

Introduction

The age in which Jane Austen lived was an age of turbulence both at home and abroad. The French Revolution that broke out in 1789 had a great impact on England, and in the subsequent years the country was off and on at war with France till the final peace of 1815. On the other hand, owing to the progress of the Industrial Revolution English society in this period was changing rapidly in its structure. In recent years the relationship between Jane Austen's works and the contemporary society has indeed become the main focus of interest in Austen scholarship, but formerly her works were considered to be quite independent of the din and tumult of the times. G. M. Trevelyan, a leading historian of the first half of the twentieth century, evidently regarded her novels as such. While discussing the political and economic effects of the Napoleonic Wars upon the nation, he also stresses the fact that the wars little affected the daily scenes in the English social life, and it is Jane Austen that Trevelyan adduces as a clear example of this: 'In the mirror that Miss Austen held up to nature in the drawing-room, it is hard to detect any trace of concern or trouble arising from the war'.[1] As a matter of fact, till about the middle of the previous century Jane Austen was generally regarded as a novelist who showed rare ability in portraying an ordinary life within the narrow range of the countryside, but never turned her eye to the wider world outside her province.

In the second half of the century—especially from the 1970s onward—the attempt to grasp Jane Austen's novels in historical context became the main stream of the criticism, and various aspects and trends of the contemporary society began to be associated with the world of her novels. From much earlier Jane Austen, who seems to accept implicitly the traditional values and system of her society, tended to be regarded as a conservative writer; but in the early 1970s Alistair M. Duckworth researched minutely into the social conditions of the times and discussed Jane Austen's stance in a more demonstrative way. The gentry who stand at the top of local communities play a pivotal role in the maintenance of social order; in the rapidly changing society, therefore, they need to 'improve' themselves—that is, to adjust themselves to the developments—in order to preserve the necessary qualification for leaders—this, so Duckworth argues, is the message woven into the novels.[2] The image of the novelist as a Burkean conservative was thus put forward, and Duckworth's approach took the initiative in those kinds of studies which explore the historical and political dimensions of her novels. In the bicentenary year of Jane Austen's birth Marilyn Butler represented her as a novelist with keen political awareness. Putting her novels against the context of 'the war of ideas', Butler placed them directly in the company of anti-Jacobin novels of the 1790s.[3] In contrast to these studies, the rise of the feminist criticism in the 1980s brought about a very adverse view of the novelist. Ranging extensively over the literary and other works of this period, Claudia L. Johnson found in the novels numerous elements which had a close affinity with the progressive and radical ideas of the day.[4] Conservative as she may appear on the surface, Jane Austen's stance was essentially subversive—this on the whole is the assertion of feminist scholars.

In her novels (and anywhere else, too, for that matter) Jane Austen never expressed anything like political beliefs or philosophies, so that it is possible, in a sense, to attribute any kind of credo to her. Yet one cannot help wondering at the readings of the novels so opposite to each other. At the same time, such views as that Jane Austen fluctuated between conservatism and radicalism are easy compromises and far from satisfactory. The Austen studies in and after the 1970s have had a definite significance in that they have demonstrated the close link between her works and the contemporary society; many of them, however, have put the novelist in a particular ideological or political stance, and obviously the problem lies there. It is indeed undeniable that Jane Austen observed her society widely and closely, and her observations were evidently reflected in her novels; but it is doubtful whether she attempted to advocate any particular doctrine or belief through her works—they were certainly not written for political or propaganda purpose. For what purpose, then, did Jane Austen write the novels? To consider the question it would be helpful to examine how she handles the matter of social conventions which reflect the system and ideology of a community.

> 'You are mistaken, Mr. Darcy, if you suppose that the mode of your declaration affected me in any other way, than as it spared me the concern which I might have felt in refusing you, had you behaved in a more gentleman-like manner.' (*PP* 192)

Thus Elizabeth Bennet expresses her indignation in the memorable scene of her spirited repulse of Darcy's proposal. Astonished as she is at the offer of this 'proud' man, she is more incensed by the insolent manner of his speech, which leads to this pungent reproof. Elizabeth enumerates several reasons for disliking Darcy, but this flat condemnation of his incivility most bitterly pierces his heart. Indeed, in Jane Austen's world the observance of the conventional rules of propriety is a matter of no trivial importance, and deviation from those rules is seldom tolerated, whether it is perpetrated thoughtlessly or deliberately. In Darcy's case, his deviation is quite unwitting; he has been sometimes even critical of Elizabeth's bold behaviour, and this unexpected attack on his own lack of civility shatters his 'pride'. Marianne Dashwood, on the other hand, disregards the social code on her own principles. Her habitual rudeness is the worry of her sister Elinor, but her audacious behaviour sometimes engages our sympathy. In the episode of the dinner party at John Dashwood's house, Mrs Ferrars and Fanny Dashwood attempt to mortify Elinor by malicious insinuations, and Marianne, unable to bear such an affront to her sister, warmly protests against the insulting ladies. Yet this indecorous manifestation of her sisterly affection is coolly received by Elinor, who 'was much more hurt by Marianne's warmth, than she had been by what produced it' (*SS* 236). The importance of conformity to the conventional rules of conduct is perhaps more pointedly stressed in *Sense and Sensibility* than in the other works—indeed, what harm would arise from the disregard of rules is the central theme of the novel—but, in any case, certainly nowhere in her novels does Jane Austen encourage anti-social behaviour.

Of course outward conformity to the proprieties does not necessarily indicate inward moral integrity, and examples of 'deceitful good manners' abound in Jane Austen's novels. Elizabeth, who is ready to denounce Darcy's haughty manner, is equally ready to be imposed on by Wickham's 'excess of good breeding' (*PP* 73), and Emma at first extols Elton's manners as 'a model' (*E* 34). But this unreliability of outward manners by no means lessens the importance of rules themselves. Jane Austen was well aware that rules of behaviour were closely bound up with social order; in the theatrical episode in *Mansfield Park* we find a vivid representation of anarchy resulting from the disappearance of the proprieties. Rules of behaviour are things inevitable and indispensable in human society—this is an implicit premise in Jane Austen's world, and from this very premise arises her drama. If the observance of the established rules ensures the preservation of order in society, it does not solve every problem that accompanies the individual's life in society; on the contrary, many complicated problems proceed from the unavoidable existence of rules, and one of them is the problem of deceitful good manners. Not only Elizabeth and Emma but almost all the heroines of Jane Austen's novels have to face the difficulty of penetrating reality beneath plausible appearance. How to preserve self-respect without infringing laws of society is the problem that confronts Marianne Dashwood. Holding in contempt the mediocre people among whom she is obliged to live, Marianne disdains to comply with the conventional rules of conduct they willingly and perhaps blindly follow; for her compliance with those rules means subjection to the foolish neighbours. Yet such vaulting arrogance is to involve her in painful ordeals. Marianne's struggles do illustrate the difficulty intellectuals are liable to experience in reconciling the demands of the individual to those of society.

One essential aspect of the social code in which Jane Austen took a keen interest is its mutability. Anne Elliot, when she visits her sister Mary at Uppercross, realizes anew that 'a removal from one set of people to another, though at a distance of only three miles, will often include a total change of conversation, opinion, and idea' (*P* 42). Indeed, the way of life at Uppercross is so different from that at Kellynch that every time she visits there she has to make a conscious effort to adapt herself to the Musgrove ways. Along with this instance of Anne, another episode in the novels that reminds us that manners and customs vary by group is Fanny Price's return to Portsmouth in *Mansfield Park*. Actually, the difference in way of life between Mansfield and Portsmouth is even greater than that between Kellynch and Uppercross, and Fanny's reaction to the drastic change in life habits is one noteworthy point in the episode. In her father's house Fanny finds enough noise and confusion but no 'manners'—an indication again of the close link between propriety and order—and consequently the value of the tranquility and regularity of Mansfield Park daily increases in her mind. In spite of her growing wish to return to Mansfield, however, Fanny is obliged to stay at Portsmouth for nearly three months, and to the end she is unable to adjust herself to the lifestyle of her own family. Perhaps Fanny is rather exceptional in her lack of adaptability; yet it is not Fanny alone who is governed by 'habit'. Even Henry Crawford, who is always in pursuit of novelty, is unable after all to shake off his London habits, and so is his sister Mary—Mansfield fails to 'cure' them. And the relationship between this inflexibility of human nature and the mutability of the social code is one of the author's main concerns in the novel.

The standard of the proprieties varies, of course, not only from circle to circle but also from age to age; in fact, in Jane Austen's time the standard was fast changing. In England such changes occurred periodically. From Shakespeare's plays we can visualize the 'merry' and lively Elizabethan England; but the cheerful and open atmosphere of this age was succeeded in the seventeenth century by the rigorous and stuffy climate under the influence of Puritanism. Then in the Restoration a free—and not a little dissipated—atmosphere returned to England, which on the whole survived through the eighteenth century. Yet this wild freedom was in turn replaced in the nineteenth century by the stiff solemnity of the Victorian era. The age in which Jane Austen lived was a changeover period from the eighteenth century to the Victorian era; during this period England underwent a radical change in social customs. In 1789 the French Revolution broke out, and amid the growing alarm about the threat of Jacobinism the importance of manners as an indispensable factor in maintaining order and peace in society was recognized anew. In this reactionary atmosphere a group of ardent reformers carried on energetic campaigns to improve manners and morals, which achieved a notable success by the time the Regency began. The sober atmosphere that pervades the world of Mansfield Park is obviously a reflection of the new serious social climate of the 1810s, and how such rapid transformation in social customs affects the individual—and society as well—is an important theme of the novel. As the scenes of chaotic disturbance which appear more than once in the novel imply, Jane Austen by no means favourably regarded that situation in her society.

Jane Austen was also well aware that one particular set of rules of propriety was founded on one particular ideology. In *Pride and Prejudice* there is an episode in which Elizabeth walks alone across muddy fields to Netherfield Park to look after her sick sister Jane. This walk exposes her to ridicule and criticism when she arrives there; the most merciless is Miss Bingley, who condemns it as 'an abominable sort of conceited independence, a most country town indifference to decorum' (*PP* 36). Similar censure on woman's audacity is found in a more serious scene; when Fanny refuses Henry Crawford's proposal, Sir Thomas accuses her of 'wilfulness of temper, self-conceit, and . . . that independence of spirit, which prevails so much in modern days, even in young women, and which in young women is offensive and disgusting beyond all common offence' (*MP* 318). One notices that in either case the reproach itself is a sort of disguise, intentional or unintentional; there is jealousy towards Elizabeth behind Caroline Bingley's bitterness, and Sir Thomas's accusation is quite unreasonable, springing solely from the frustrated ambition. Whether just or not, however, their reproaches—the terms they employ—indicate the prevalence of a certain ideological assumption which demands modesty and obedience from women, and on which are built the current rules of propriety; and this assumption is so firmly rooted in people's mind in Jane Austen's world—there is actually no one who dares to call it into question—that any deviation from those rules which are based on it is regarded as an 'offence'. Needless to say, the assumption was generally accepted in the society in which Jane Austen lived. But how did Jane Austen herself take the matter? Were her views accordant with the dominant ideology of her society?

Women in Jane Austen's novels are on the whole in a vulnerable position, economically and socially. They are often obliged to give way to men; owing to the 'entail' the Bennet girls are deprived of the right to inherit their father's estate, and the Dashwood sisters have to hand over the inheritance of Norland Park to their half brother, to whom 'the succession to the Norland estate was not so really important as to his sisters' (*SS* 3), and who, at the instigation of his wife, practically turns them out of Norland. A woman's status in society depends almost entirely on how she marries (hence the pressing importance of marriage to women in the novels); an unmarried woman with little money, therefore, 'must be a ridiculous, disagreeable, old maid', as Emma observes (*E* 85). 'Reputation' of a woman is very fragile; fatal consequences inevitably ensue from women's sexual misconduct, while men's goes with comparative impunity. Thus for the same crime Maria Rushworth suffers severer punishment than Henry Crawford, and it is also the case with Eliza the daughter and Willoughby—the existence of 'double standards' is palpable there. Although Jane Austen never complains openly of women's vulnerability or articulates a protest against sexual inequality, there seems to be an undercurrent of criticism in their description towards the patriarchal ideology which connives at or even promotes those kinds of injustice. All the same, Jane Austen manifests no wish to deny the efficacy of the conventional rules of propriety, even though they are the offsprings of that unreasonable ideology. Perhaps she was caught in a dilemma, but it seems that her respect for rules was never substantially undermined. There was the problem of 'order', for one thing, and in this respect the French Revolution provided striking object lessons; the bloody disasters which occurred during progress of the revolution warned her, no doubt, of the danger that must necessarily accompany the total abolition of laws of society, however unjust those laws might be. For another, the welfare of the individual is in fact as much dependent on the existence of rules as that of society is—so she considered, and in *Sense and Sensibility* she gives an acute insight into the relationship between rules of behaviour and the individual's emotional welfare. Jane Austen certainly did not regard the rules of propriety current in her society as the best set of rules (at the same time, she probably doubted the existence of such things as the best rules); but she did not disregard the importance of rules either. Perhaps this is what most distinguishes Jane Austen from radicals of her days—and from radicals of modern days, too, for that matter.

Elizabeth clothes her reproach in the phraseology: 'had you behaved in a more gentleman-like manner'. These words not merely express her objection to Darcy's incivility; they carry an obvious implication that he lacks—or has failed to cultivate—the qualities requisite to a 'gentleman'. Her words are to all intents and purposes a denial of his gentlemanship, and this is what 'tortures' him (as he later calls it) more than her refusal itself. He is tortured, but not enraged; admitting the justice of her reproof, he repents his conceited arrogance, the result of which appears in his 'civility' which repeatedly surprises Elizabeth in Derbyshire. Yet it is not his altered manner alone that impresses her there. Although Darcy's letter has dispelled her misunderstanding concerning Wickham, doubt has obviously lingered in her mind about his character as a gentleman. At Pemberley, however, she is surprised to hear him described by the housekeeper as 'the best landlord, and the best master . . . that ever lived' (*PP* 249). 'As a brother, a landlord, a master, she considered how many people's happiness were in his guardianship!—How much of pleasure or pain it was in his power to bestow!—How much of good or evil must be done by him!'—thus reflecting, Elizabeth appreciates the grave responsibilities that appertain to his position (*PP* 250–51), and Mrs Reynolds' assurance that he is a faithful discharger of all those responsibilities deeply affects her mind. With her respect for him thus increasing, she feels 'gratitude' for 'his regard': 'she remembered its warmth, and softened its impropriety of expression' (*PP* 251). At Pemberley Elizabeth realizes that, important as they certainly are, good manners are by no means the only necessary qualification for a gentleman. And what are the necessary qualifications for a gentleman is indeed a matter of grave importance in Jane Austen's novels.

Harold Perkin describes English society in Jane Austen's time as 'a hierarchical society in which men took their places in an accepted order of precedence, a pyramid stretching down from a tiny minority of the rich and powerful through ever larger and wider layers of lesser wealth and power to the great mass of the poor and powerless'.[5] There were indeed numerous 'ranks' or 'degrees' which strictly defined people's positions in the hierarchy, but no 'classes' yet; it was in the years after Waterloo that classes in the sense of mutually hostile layers united by common interests and common source of income came to the surface in English society. In general, there was until then no hostility or antagonism between people in different ranks; rather, they were closely linked with one another vertically. In such society the role of landowners who stood at the top of the hierarchy—the 'tiny minority of the rich and powerful'—was particularly important. Since the power of the government then was confined in such spheres as the maintenance of law and order and the management of foreign affairs, the landed gentry enjoyed exclusive authority in the countryside. It is not, however, that landowners ruled their communities oppressively; the nature of the gentry's dominion over village life was not so much dictatorship as paternalism. It was commonly held that landowners' privileges—superiority of birth, wealth, leisure and education—were given to them mainly to serve the public, and on the whole the English gentry had a strong sense of responsibility and fulfilled their role as leaders of communities; indeed, they were 'the major pillar of stability in a world which, bereft of their influence and control, would dissolve into uncertainty, lawlessness, and chaos'.[6] Jane Austen gives a vivid picture of life in a rural community in *Emma*, and Mr Knightley, an active and benevolent landowner, could be seen as an exemplar of the gentry of this period.

One is inclined to ask whether Jane Austen approved of the hierarchical system of her society unconditionally. But we should be careful in asking this question, as we should be careful in asking whether she approved of the patriarchal system of her society; for, in either case, if we engross ourselves too much in the right or wrong of the system or in her attitude towards it, we are likely to miss an essential aspect of her novels. Jane Austen's concern in writing novels lay, above all else, in demonstrating the basic mechanisms of human society, and this is one reason why she so scrupulously avoided references to the contemporary political issues, home or abroad. Incidents and phenomena, such as the French Revolution or the English reaction to it, no doubt attracted her notice; indeed, they were the very things that gave her an insight into the mechanisms; yet she had no wish to participate in the political controversies of the day—no wish to fight for some particular cause or advocate some particular ideology. Her interest was directed more towards extracting from those incidents and phenomena the general principles that governed man's life in society. As for the hierarchical system of her society, perhaps she felt the injustice of social inequality, just as she felt the injustice of sexual inequality, but denunciation of such injustice was by no means her purpose in writing novels; rather, aware of the inevitability of hierarchy in human society, as she was aware of the indispensability of rules of behaviour, she was more absorbed in the problem of how hierarchy functioned than in the problem of how just its particular instance was. Hence comes the importance of gentlemen's conduct in Jane Austen's novels; she fully realized that the proper operation of hierarchy depended first and foremost on those who stood at the top of it, and that their misconduct would directly affect the welfare of society.

In the hierarchical society persons belonging to privileged classes were expected to give generous help to the underprivileged. In *Emma* there is a scene in which Emma pays a charity visit to a poor sick family with Harriet. Emma is a member—or a 'mistress'—of a family who are 'first in consequence' in Highbury (*E* 7); it is incumbent on her therefore to do this kind of charitable act. Emma believes that she understands her duty well; yet in the course of time her understanding proves to be deficient, and this deficiency has a close relationship with a certain tendency she exhibits—a tendency to dissimulate her motives. In her officious efforts to make a match between Harriet and Elton, she persuades herself into believing that she is acting for Harriet's sake. In fact, however, Emma's match-making project is motivated by her own inclinations and conveniences which have nothing to do with Harriet; but she would not admit this to herself and, instead, always pleads Harriet's advantage. The scheme itself ends comically with the unexpected offer of marriage to herself by Elton; yet, considering her position in society, this tendency to self-delusion is by no means comical.

Besides Emma, Jane Austen portrays several characters who have the similar habit of dissembling their real motives—such as General Tilney, Darcy, and Sir Thomas Bertram. In the following pages we shall examine in detail the ways they deceive themselves to justify their conduct, and here we just note the repeated portrayal of this type of behaviour pattern in the novels. Jane Austen well knew the danger involved in this kind of rationalization; in France in the 1790s savage slaughter was perpetrated in the name of Revolution. Of course in her novels she does not depict such atrocities; with a penetrating insight into the workings of the human mind, however, she seems to warn us that grim consequences might arise when it works wrong. Significantly, those who show the tendency to the self-deception are all persons in an influential position. As Elizabeth realizes at Pemberley, 'many people's happiness' rests on these persons' 'guardianship'; it is in their power to bestow 'much pain' as well as 'much pleasure'; indeed, whether 'much good' or 'much evil' is done depends on their conduct. Jane Austen draws a number of 'irresponsible' gentlemen; Henry Crawford spends so little time at his own estate that he little knows what is going on there, and Sir Walter Elliot, owing to his snobbish extravagance, is obliged to let his seat, Kellynch Hall. But in a sense irresponsibility is less harmful than responsibility misdirected; negligence is less pernicious than misplaced enthusiasm. In the name of 'kindness' Emma severs Harriet from a suitable man, and the other gentlemen also betray a similar propensity to unjust or cruel control of others (Emma's 'kindness' is unwelcome to the community as well—her arbitrary raising of Harriet's status is an act which disturbs the order in the hierarchy). Thus the self-absorption in a person in authority is apt to affect the welfare of many; indeed, the 'guardianship' is transformed unwittingly into a 'menace' to society. That Jane Austen repeatedly portrayed self-deceiving persons of consequence points, it seems, to her deep anxiety about this sinister tendency, and that her anxiety was not exaggerated has been amply proved by history.

CHAPTER 1

General Tilney and Tyranny:
Northanger Abbey

Northanger Abbey falls short of Catherine Morland's expectations from the first. At the entrance to its grounds, the lodges she passes through present 'a modern appearance' (161); the furniture of the drawing room she is shown into is 'in all the profusion and elegance of modern taste' (162). Indeed, Northanger Abbey turns out to be far from what Catherine's eager imagination has pictured to herself, and the contrast between her expectation of 'a fine old place' (157) and the glaring newness which everywhere meets her eye heightens the comical effect of the Abbey scenes in the novel. This contrast, however, serves not merely to expose the naivety of a girl addicted to novels; it also highlights the peculiar inclinations of General Tilney, the owner of Northanger, who has transformed an ancient abbey into a place for exhibiting modern products and inventions. The General's love of improvement and novelty is indeed almost as obsessive as Catherine's yearning for ruins and antiquities. Catherine's naivety is also revealed through her fantastic adventures; fancifully identifying the General with such fictional villains as Montoni, she looks for evidence of imaginary guilt. But this confusion of fiction and reality, too, while testifying to her simplicity, proves to be an illuminating comment on the character of the General as an avaricious despot. *Northanger Abbey* is admittedly the story of Catherine—of her education through her various experiences. On the other hand, General Tilney deserves our close attention in his own right; he by no means functions merely as a subject of Catherine's study. If he is a man of mystery—a puzzle to solve—to Catherine, so he is to the modern reader. The General has a passion for improvement and novelty, and Jane Austen underlines his enthusiasm by describing his possessions and activities with a degree of minuteness rather unusual for her. But what is her purpose in doing so? Is it only to laugh at the vanity of a wealthy, worldly-minded landowner? Along with these questions, we must consider carefully why the General is connected with Gothic villains. Catherine's Gothic adventures are a little out of tune with the rest of the book, and there must have been some important reason that the author should risk such dissonance. Jane Austen certainly implies more about the General than she makes explicit; to grasp her meaning it is necessary to find links between the several images associated with the General and contemporary political and social conditions, and his character as a domestic autocrat is a key to the complicated message the author tries to convey through this personage.

Jane Austen twice uses the word 'tyranny'. In the opening paragraph we are told that Catherine 'was seldom stubborn, scarcely ever quarrelsome, and very kind to the little ones, with few interruptions of tyranny' (14). And in the closing passage, which parodies the moralizing cliché of contemporary novels, we find the phrase 'parental tyranny' (252). 'Parental tyranny' refers, of course, to General Tilney. He is indeed a despot, 'accustomed on every ordinary occasion to give the law in his family' (247). His binding authority is such that he is 'always a check upon his children's spirits' (156). As a character he is rather simplified; described from outside and with exaggeration, General Tilney may be called a caricature or a 'flat' character, Yet Jane Austen's representation of his despotism is subtle. Alistair Duckworth observes that his domestic tyranny is revealed in his exacting demand of punctuality from his family; he betrays an extraordinary degree of impatience and irritation with any delay, and certainly 'his obsessive attitude toward time' as Duckworth puts it, bespeaks his inexorable martinettish disposition.[1] But more than this, all the essential characteristics of tyranny are quite skilfully embodied in General Tilney; and when we combine his tyrannical personality with the images associated with him, this caricatured figure begins to assume a grave and even sinister character.

In the 'Advertisement' to *Northanger Abbey*, written in 1816 in preparation for its publication, Jane Austen requests the reader to bear in mind that the work, while finished in 1803, was begun much earlier, and the social background belongs to the period of its original composition. This note is testimony to Jane Austen's scrupulous regard for accuracy of detail in her works; along with her concern for the fidelity of her portrait of society, however, perhaps there was some necessity for her to inform readers that the novel is set in the late 1790s. In fact, the historical context of the 1790s plays an important role in *Northanger Abbey*.

The 1790s in England was marked by the alarm caused by the political upheaval in France. The outbreak of the French Revolution in 1789 shook England profoundly, and as the Revolution proceeded its impact on English life grew even stronger. The escalation of violence, from the September Massacres in 1792 to the Reign of Terror in 1793–94, aroused intense fears. The English people not only shuddered at the bloody incidents in France but were afraid that these would spread by contagion to England. In the early 1790s London was at times disturbed by riots, and, if the Jacobins were not actually concerned in them, it was widely believed that they were. And in 1795 there were large-scale and highly seditious gatherings of radicals, such as the one in St George's Field. The 1790s was indeed a period of unrest. The Pitt government adopted rigorous measures to repress the activities of radicals, which were fairly successful; but the subversive tension that permeated the nation could not be wholly dispelled. We can glimpse this atmosphere of anxiety in *Northanger Abbey*. In chapter 14, during the course of the walk on Beechen Cliff, Eleanor Tilney mistakes Catherine's remark about a forthcoming horror novel for a reference to an impending riot, and her brother Henry, amused at her misapprehension, makes fun of her by giving a facetious description of a London riot. Considering the actual state of affairs in the 1790s, however, Eleanor is by no means over-imaginative, nor is Henry's representation of a riot an unrealistic fairy tale, as he tries to make it appear. As B. C. Southam observes, 'Eleanor's misunderstanding and Tilney's joke touch upon circumstances bizarrely close to the truth' of the time.²

The 1790s was also a period in which the Gothic novel had an enormous vogue. This interesting phenomenon may be traced back to various causes—there were backgrounds, literary, intellectual, and social; among the rest, one important factor that undoubtedly contributed to its vogue was the impact of the French Revolution. Ronald Paulson points out that 'the popularity of Gothic fiction in the 1790s and well into the nineteenth century was due in part to the widespread anxieties and fears in Europe aroused by the turmoil in France'.³ Actually, the anxieties and fears which marked this period are also the salient features of Gothic fiction, especially the works of the Radcliffean school. Ann Radcliffe, the most popular and influential Gothic novelist of the time, presents heroines who are in some way or other persecuted by ruthless villains; in *The Mysteries of Udolpho*, for example, the heroine Emily is imprisoned in the castle Udolpho by the avaricious and cruel desperado Montoni. Paulson remarks: 'By the time *The Mysteries of Udolpho* appeared (1794), the castle, prison, tyrant, and sensitive young girl could no longer be presented naively; they had all been familiarized and sophisticated by the events in France'.⁴ A sensitive young girl and a savage tyrant are stock characters in Gothic novels, and the strength of Radcliffe's works—and those of her imitators—lies, among other things, in the suspense created over the fate of the imprisoned heroine who is constantly threatened with violence. Indeed, the image of an innocent girl seized with anxieties and fears under the threat of violence by an oppressive villain 'bizarrely' overlapped the image of England in the 1790s, and the contemporary reader could not be blind to that. The Gothic novel has often been regarded as an escape from reality, but the reality of the day in fact propelled the terror of its fiction.

Gothic villains, then, were seen as emblems of the French menace, and this image was presumably the more readily accepted for several traits they exhibit which particularly evoked the French revolutionaries. Villains in Gothic novels are in many cases slaves to their passions. In *Udolpho* Emily is warned by her father against 'excessive indulgence', and her moderation is juxtaposed with 'the wild energy of passion' of Montoni, a man 'in whom passions . . . entirely supplied the place of principles'.⁵

Such unrestrained passion is characteristic, not only of Montoni, but of almost every other villain of Gothic fiction, and, as Paulson points out, 'the "wild energy" of Montoni is what Burke associates with the French rabble'.[6] Together with unbridled passion, Gothic villains are also linked to the Revolution in their assumption of unlimited power. Criticizing the drastic measures taken in France, Burke remarks that if the 'engagement and pact of society' are set at nought, 'competence and power would soon be confounded, and no law be left but the will of a prevailing force'.[7] Burke's prediction about the abuse of power was soon to be realized in the Reign of Terror, and the tyranny of the Revolution bears a close analogy with the behaviour of Gothic villains, who also admit no law but their own will. It is worth noting that in committing atrocities those villains frequently try to justify themselves in an arbitrary way. In *The Romance of the Forest* (1791), for example, the Marquis de Montalt, deprecating the laws of a civilized country as 'prejudices' and 'false refinement', and alleging one's advantages or 'unconquerable' passions as ample justification for murder, enjoins La Motte to put Adeline to death. Characteristically, the Marquis calls his creed 'truth'.[8] Similarly, in Eleanor Sleath's *The Orphan of the Rhine* (1798), the Marchese de Montferrat, following the advice of his servant Paoli, decides to murder Laurette with a plea of 'self-preservation'.[9] But the most impressive example of perverted self-justification is found in the conference scene between the Marchesa di Vivaldi and Father Schedoni in *The Italian* (1797). Both the Marchesa and Schedoni have reasons—egoistic, more or less—for wanting to get rid of Ellena Rosalba, the lady-love of the Marchesa's son, and in this murder-plotting scene the Marchesa allows herself to be persuaded by the sophistry of Schedoni, who calls Ellena's murder 'justice' or 'virtue'.[10] In *The Italian*, the Inquisition also plays the role of oppressive villain. In the prison of the Inquisition Vivaldi is filled with 'astonishment and indignation of the sufferings, which the frenzied wickedness of man prepares for man, who, even at the moment of infliction, insults his victim with assertions of the justice and necessity of such procedure'.[11] The readers of the 1790s would have associated such abuse of power, particularly when accompanied by far-fetched self-justification, with the slaughter perpetrated in France in the name of Revolution; Vivaldi's astonishment and indignation at the inhumanity of the Inquisition represents English emotions about the tyranny of the Revolution.

Seen against this background, the comparison of General Tilney with Gothic villains takes on a greater significance, even though the comparison is made by the naive Catherine. The General is not a murderer, nor does he confine his wife, as Catherine imagines; but her comparison is amply justified by his final 'violence'—her abrupt dismissal from Northanger, which is indeed the finishing touch to his portrait as a domestic tyrant. When Henry enlightens her as to the reasons for his father's conduct, Catherine feels 'that in suspecting General Tilney of either murdering or shutting up his wife, she had scarcely sinned against his character, or magnified his cruelty' (247). If, therefore, the novel had been published when the author originally intended—at a time when the bloody incidents in France were still vivid in the people's minds—then it would not have been difficult for the contemporary reader to perceive the shadow of the tyranny of the Revolution behind the dictatorial General Tilney. I do not mean to suggest, however, that the General is a radical or revolutionary. Jane Austen projected the image of the violence of the Revolution on the General in order to intimate the horror of tyranny; the French Revolution afforded a glaring and graphic example.

Tyranny, however, was by no means a monopoly of France; the Revolution in France gave rise to what might be termed a reactionary tyranny in England. As we have seen, the government tried to repress the subversive movements, and the measures they took were indeed severe. In 1793 and 1794 leaders of radical groups were arrested and tried, some transported; in 1794 Habeas Corpus was temporarily suspended, making possible the imprisonment of political suspects without trial; steps were taken in legislation, including the Treasonable Practices Act and the Seditious Meetings Act of 1795, which notably restricted the activities of dissidents.[12] In parallel with these proceedings of the authorities, voluntary movements of citizens also developed. In 1792 John Reeves, a legal historian, founded the Association for the Preservation of Liberty and Property against Republicans and Levellers in order to conduct a reactionary campaign. The activities of the Association were supported by the government, but the general public also co-operated. Under the leadership of the Association, local societies, organized 'in every quarter of the nation', were zealous 'to move against seditious meetings and publications, to bring offenders to justice', and 'to stand in readiness to aid the executive power and magistrates in the suppression of any riots or tumults'.[13]

Owing to their success, the associations themselves were soon to dissolve; yet the habit of local citizens volunteering information about seditious activities remained, and was made use of by the government. E.P. Thompson remarks that, in order to stifle the activities of reformers, 'the authorities were prompted to employ spies and informers on a scale unknown in any other period'. The information furnished tended to be exaggerated or even fabricated, but the government encouraged it: 'To isolate and terrorize potential revolutionaries, it was possible to adopt a policy of deliberate provocation'.[14] As a result, England was filled with an extremely repressive atmosphere. In *The Friend* Coleridge wrote: 'in England, when the alarm was at the highest, there was not a city, no, not a town in which a man suspected of holding democratic principles could move abroad without receiving some unpleasant proof of the hatred in which his supposed opinions were held by the great majority of the people'.[15] Actually, as he relates in the tenth chapter of his *Biographia Literaria*, in Somerset, in 1796, he and Wordsworth, suspected of being Jacobins, were reported to the government by local residents.[16] As Southam and Warren Roberts point out, there was a political and social background behind Henry Tilney's famous observation that England is a country 'where every man is surrounded by a neighbourhood of voluntary spies' (198).[17]

In relation to the political atmosphere of the 1790s, Robert Hopkins propounds a very interesting view of General Tilney.[18] After touring the grounds and the Abbey, at the close of the evening when the others are going to retire, the General announces, somewhat pompously, his intention of sitting up a little longer:

> 'I have many pamphlets to finish,' said he to Catherine, 'before I can close my eyes; and perhaps may be poring over the affairs of

the nation for hours after you are asleep. Can either of us be more meetly employed? *My* eyes will be blinding for the good of others; and *yours* preparing by rest for future mischief.' (187)

This nightly duty of the General is mysterious enough to induce the fanciful Catherine to suspect that the pamphlet-reading is a hocus-pocus pretence to cover some dark proceedings, and to the modern reader its nature is also a puzzle. Hopkins maintains, however, that 'had *Northanger Abbey* been published in the late 1790s or early 1800s Jane Austen's readers would have instantly caught the significance of the General's duties'.[19] In view of the historical context of this period we have just seen, he concludes that 'General Tilney's duties at night were as an inquisitor surveying possibly seditious pamphlets';[20] the General, that is, is one of the 'voluntary spies'. Hopkins's hypothesis is ingenious and entirely tenable; the General's character and the contemporary political and social conditions support this proposition. Although it may appear inconsistent with his revolutionary image to see the General as a reactionary patriot who volunteers to take action against Jacobinism (indeed, just before that pamphlet-reading passage Catherine perceives in the gloomily pacing General 'the air and attitude of a Montoni'), this is not necessarily so; the Revolution and the Reaction—these extremes meet in tyranny. If the brutal violence in France was one extreme manifestation of tyranny, the stern repression of revolutionary or reform movements in England was another. Coleridge remarks that 'to withstand the arguments of the lawless, the Anti-jacobins proposed to suspend the Law, and by the interposition of a particular statute to eclipse the blessed light of the universal Sun, that spies and informers might tyrannize and escape in the ominous darkness'.[21] Indeed, the spy-system and the fanatic patriotism of those voluntary spies can be regarded as a symbol of the political repression of this period. Jane Austen subtly projects the image of those patriots onto General Tilney to remind her readers of the actual nightmarish tyranny of their own country.

Thus the Reaction, like the Revolution, offered an illustrative example of tyranny, and General Tilney, on whom their images converge, offers an illustration of the essential characteristic—or mechanism, one may say—of tyranny common to both of them. In the pamphlet-reading passage the General says: '*My* eyes will be blinding for the good of others'. If his nightly duty is to inspect pamphlet literature for seditious contents, the phrase 'for the good of others' takes on a sinister connotation; it suggests an attitude peculiar to tyranny—the holding up of a banner of a noble cause. It is indeed customary for the General to allege some specious reasons—the benefit of others or their convenience—rather than his own desires or intentions when he tries to carry his point. He invites Catherine to Northanger Abbey for mercenary reasons, yet he does so as if for the sake of his daughter Eleanor. When, deferring showing her round the Abbey, he takes Catherine outdoors, it is because he wishes to take the air at his usual hour; yet he says he yields to her desire as if it were against his own inclination. These are trivial examples, but they afford a glimpse into the working of his mind. For a man like the General a cause supplies a pretext and a cover: a pretext to impose one's will, opinions, or principles; and a cover to conceal selfish purposes, from oneself as well as from others. Indeed, we could say that the self-deception or self-absorption under the pretext of some worthy cause is an attribute of tyranny, and those who believe themselves fighting for a great cause are capable of any action, however outrageous or cruel that action may be. General Tilney's behaviour pattern illustrates this mechanism of tyranny, and Jane Austen believed that fundamentally the same mechanism was at work in the political world of both France and England in the 1790s.

But tyranny is not necessarily a phenomenon peculiar to the political world. In the society of this period where industry was developing rapidly, Jane Austen perceived another form of tyranny spreading, and it is again in General Tilney that this tyranny is incarnated. In the scenes of the conducted tour of the grounds and the Abbey various things are shown to Catherine one after another—an enormous kitchen garden, gorgeous household equipment, objects of domestic utility, and so on. These are treated with considerable detail, and Southam, taking notice of this unusual minuteness, insists upon the necessity of historical insight into the matter.[22] To grasp its full meaning it is necessary to understand how the gentry concerned themselves with and contributed to the development of industry in the late eighteenth and early nineteenth centuries. It has been argued that in Jane Austen's novels the landowning classes are represented as degenerating and losing strength, and their decline—economic as well as moral—is usually contrasted with the vitality and new virtues of the rising middle classes. Yet David Spring asserts that this view is not founded on historical reality.[23] According to him, eighteenth-century English landowners were far from being effete; they were powerful as a governing class, and were to remain so throughout the nineteenth century. Moreover, as a businesslike, capitalist class, they were making remarkable progress economically. During the Beechen Cliff episode Henry Tilney refers to 'the inclosure' in 'his short disquisition on the state of the nation' (111). The late eighteenth century was in fact a period in which the enclosure movement was at its height, and this movement enhanced the economic prosperity of landowners; enclosure not only increased their estates but also enlivened their businesslike activities. On their enlarged estates they carried out extensive improvements in agriculture and their success brought them large profits. Indeed, they were quite assiduous in pursuing profit, and in this respect had much in common with merchants and manufacturers. Landowners by no means swam against the current; rather, they made an important contribution to industrial development. Spring writes:

> Although English landowners were not commercial or industrial capitalists, they were agrarian capitalists. In their own sphere, they were economic modernizers, in no important sense hostile to other spheres of economic modernity; on the contrary, by reason of the importance of agriculture in the national economy, they helped mightily in generating England's pioneering achievement, the industrial revolution, and managed as well to derive profit from it.[24]

The landowning classes, then, making common cause with the middle classes, took the lead in the industrial revolution. Putting particular emphasis on their acquisitive attitude, Spring remarks that 'theirs was a capitalist money culture'.[25]

Now, among the many landowners in Jane Austen's novels, none lives up to Spring's description better than General Tilney. His estate is extensive, including Woodston as well as Northanger, and he boasts to Catherine that his eldest son Frederick 'will perhaps inherit as considerable a landed property as any private man in the country' (176). The extent of his estate is symbolized by the kitchen garden, whose vast scale astounds Catherine:

> The number of acres contained in this garden was such as Catherine could not listen to without dismay. . . . The walls seemed countless in number, endless in length; a village of hot-houses seemed to arise among them, and a whole parish to be at work within the inclosure. (178)

The significant use of the word 'inclosure' here, when coupled with Henry's earlier reference to the enclosure movement, might imply that the General has increased his estate by enclosure. And then the General professes himself a sympathizer with modern industry and a supporter of its development. He chose Staffordshire porcelain for his breakfast set because he 'thought it right to encourage the manufacture of his country'; but this set, purchased two years ago; he calls 'quite an old set', as '[t]he manufacture was much improved since that time' (175). Indeed, his passion for novelty is such that his life is crammed with products of modern industry; he travels in a fashionable chaise-and-four, fits up rooms with furniture of the latest fashion, and installs modern contrivances, such as a Rumford fireplace in the drawing-room and succession-houses in the kitchen garden. His neophilia extends even to food and drink; he drinks cocoa, and grows pineapples in the modern-equipped kitchen garden. He shows off all these things not only proudly but also in a coercive manner, extorting admiration and praise from Catherine for each of them, till she becomes 'heartily weary of seeing and wondering' (179). It is worth noting that here too the General now and again alleges he acts 'for the good of others'. About the rearing of fruits he pleads thus: 'Though careless enough in most matters of eating, he loved good fruit—*or if he did not, his friends and children did* (178; emphasis added). When he shows Catherine round the kitchen and offices, he tries to impress her with his benevolence towards his servants. In the kitchen his 'improving hand' has adopted 'every modern invention to facilitate the labour of the cooks' (183). As for the offices, he boasts:

> if he had a vanity, it was in the arrangement of his offices; and as he was convinced, that, to a mind like Miss Morland's, a view of the accommodations and comforts, by which the labours of her inferiors were softened, must always be gratifying, he should make no apology for leading her on. (184)[26]

The General's real vanity lies, of course, in the things themselves—rare fruit, modern inventions, new devices and equipment—or the fact that he is their introducer; 'the good of others' is little more than self-justification—and self-deception.

General Tilney's monomaniac attachment to novel commodities has often been associated with the consumer revolution of this age. Tony Tanner, for example, takes the General's 'compulsive acquisitiveness' as 'a symptom of the new consumer urge of the age and the crass material instinct for competitive emulation it spawned'.[27] Edward Copeland, on the other hand, puts emphasis on the General's snobbery rather than his acquisitiveness, seeing in it a sign of the modern consumer culture in which things are valued not for their own sake but for the prestige they confer on their possessors.[28] But whether acquisitive or snobbish, the General is regarded both by Tanner and Copeland as a type arising from the new consumer era—'a typical—and nasty—"product" of the exponential increase of consumer products which the Industrial Revolution was making available'.[29] Yet we must not forget that the General, an improving landowner, is among those who were themselves promoting industrial development—the landowning classes were leaders of the new industrial age. The General, therefore, is not a 'product' but a 'producer' of the age. According to Christopher Kent, the General is a typical example of the upper classes whose snobbery was taken advantage of by such entrepreneurs as Josiah Wedgwood—they were turned into a 'claque', praising and publicizing products of manufacturers.[30] But if they were a claque, they were a willing one. Jane Austen certainly recognized the leading position of the landed gentry in the new industrial society, and it is the way they exerted their influence that she tried to expose. They were spurred on by acquisitiveness and snobbery, yet they pleaded the benefits of industrial progress and unabashedly imposed their materialist principles upon the nation. In this attitude Jane Austen discerned tyranny, similar in essence to the other political tyrannies of this period. General Tilney's compelling materialism is an embodiment of this tyranny.

Let us here take a glance at the famous polemic passage in an earlier part of the book—the author's bold defence of the novel. In this passage Jane Austen complains of the low esteem in which the novel is generally held, and deplores especially the common practice among novelists themselves of deprecating the novel. As *Northanger Abbey* abounds in literary allusions, the passage has been commented on mainly from a literary point of view; Minako Enomoto, however, viewing the passage in a historical light, argues that Jane Austen's protest was directed in part to a group of moral reformers who exerted a vast influence upon the nation—the Evangelicals.[31] Taking advantage of the reactionary atmosphere of the 1790s, this group advocated the reformation of manners and morals on an extensive scale, and, thanks to their untiring zeal and highly organized activities, their campaigns achieved an enormous success. They were notoriously aggressive, furiously attacking whatever they considered bad and depraved, and one target among others of their attack was the novel. But there was some contradiction in the measures they took, for, while denouncing the novel as pernicious, they adopted it as a means of propagating their teachings. Hannah More's famous *Cœlebs in Search of a Wife* (1809) is a typical example. There was this background, Enomoto suggests, behind Jane Austen's harangue against novelists' disparaging of the novel. It must certainly have exasperated Jane Austen the novelist to see those who deprecate the novel unashamedly exploiting it; but perhaps what offended her most was the presumptuousness of the Evangelicals who imposed their self-approved doctrines on the nation in the name of moral reform—it must have caught her eye as a clear case of tyranny. Noting the author's tone in the passage vindicating the novel, Jane Aiken Hodge concludes that the passage was added during the final revision of the novel in 1816.[32] If so, it would not be far-fetched to suppose that Jane Austen inserted the passage to make a subtle disparagement of dictatorial reformers.

The age in which Jane Austen lived was indeed prolific in tyranny in its extreme forms, and in *Northanger Abbey* she made subtle allusions to some notable instances of tyranny which she witnessed. Yet it was by no means her intention to attack or denounce any particular instance of tyranny; she alludes to concrete examples in order to demonstrate the variety, frequency, and perniciousness of tyranny. At the same time, by weaving images of real tyranny into the character of General Tilney, she hints that all forms of tyranny are analogous, however dissimilar they may appear in their outward manifestations. It is therefore beside the mark—not to say erroneous—to read the novel as criticism of, say, the tyranny of patriarchy. Jane Austen regards tyranny primarily as a problem of human nature, rather than of systems or institutions. She knew that impetuous prescriptions against one phenomenon of tyranny were of little avail and even dangerous. In human society tyranny could take manifold forms; yet an analogy can always be drawn between one form of tyranny and another, since every variety of tyranny has its root in the soil of human nature—this is the author's message in the novel.

❧

Let us finally consider characters other than General Tilney in their relation to the theme of tyranny. *Northanger Abbey* has often been criticized as clumsily constructed, and the continuity of the story is certainly somewhat broken as the scene changes from Bath to Northanger. The characters and their actions described in the earlier part of the book, however, sometimes anticipate, and sometimes supply a contrast to, the arbitrariness of General Tilney revealed in the latter part. Isabella and John Thorpe stick at nothing to get their way, and are capable of unwarrantable coercion, as in the scene in which they, together with James Morland, press Catherine to join them in a drive to Clifton. In this episode these three—more or less prompted by selfish purposes—force Catherine to bend to their will in spite of her prior engagement. Although trivial, their coercion foreshadows the more serious 'violence' of General Tilney. As for Isabella Thorpe, we can draw a parallel between her self-deception and the General's. Isabella is certainly faithless, selfish, and acquisitive; but, shallow and thoughtless as well, she is in no sense a wily schemer like Lady Susan or Lucy Steele. Her repeated use of sentimental cant words such as 'feeling' and 'friendship' serves not so much to deceive Catherine as to deceive herself. These words are slogans, as it were, adopted and flaunted to obliterate selfish purposes. Catherine, on the other hand, is quite conscientious in her own naive way, scrupulously trying to do what is right. After repelling the unreasonable request of the Thorpes and her brother to take part in their party, she scrutinizes her motives thus:

> Setting her own inclination apart, to have failed a second time in her engagement to Miss Tilney, to have retracted a promise voluntarily made only five minutes before, and on a false pretence too, must have been wrong. She had not been withstanding them on selfish principles alone, she had not consulted merely her own gratification . . . no, she had attended to what was due to others, and to her own character in their opinion. (101)

This scrupulous attitude is never seen in the General or Isabella, and Catherine's strict self-examination presents a striking contrast to their habitual self-deception—the cloaking of 'selfish principles' with specious slogans.

Besides Catherine, there are several characters who present a contrast to General Tilney—those who are never domineering or obtrusive. Catherine's mother, for example, when she found Catherine weary of learning music, 'did not insist on her daughters being accomplished in spite of incapacity or distaste, [and] allowed her to leave off' (14). Similarly, as guardians, the Allens are far from dictatorial. Although Mr Allen has negative opinions about young men and women driving in open carriages, it is not until Catherine asks for his advice that he speaks his mind, and even then he discourages her from giving Isabella the same advice, saying 'you had better not interfere' (105). Mrs Allen's inability to advise is made fun of, but her husband's policy might be called judicious *laissez-faire*, the reverse of General Tilney's authoritarianism. Henry Tilney also tries to refrain from influencing Catherine unduly. He must see through Isabella's character at an early stage, yet he does not interfere with Catherine's friendship with her. Even when Isabella's flirtation with Captain Tilney becomes so glaring that the worried Catherine applies to Henry for advice, he refuses to give any, trying to make Catherine judge for herself. This attitude does not fundamentally change when he admonishes Catherine about her Gothic fantasies. As for her suspicions about the General's guilt, Catherine certainly goes too far, and Henry tries to convince her of her excess there; but there is no commanding or authoritative tone in his expostulation—he reasons with her. In another scene he draws an analogy between dancing and marriage, and persistently tries to persuade Catherine of the validity of his view. Unlike the General's obtrusive harangue on the need for a profession (176), however, this is hardly an imposition of opinions; rather he subtly probes Catherine's feeling about himself—his speech is 'witty courtship', as Howard S. Babb puts it.[33] Indeed, wit is another conspicuous feature of Henry Tilney. '[T]here was an archness and pleasantry in his manner'—so the narrator comments when Catherine makes her first acquaintance with him (25), and this humorous spirit seldom deserts him. Apart from his final 'revolt' against his father, he is always cool, emotionally detached from and amused at what is going on around him. And when we consider that persons of General Tilney's type often lack this spirit, Henry's 'archness and pleasantry' might be regarded as an oblique comment on tyranny.

As to the humorous spirit, however, we must not forget Jane Austen herself. In this novel she takes up the problem of tyranny with serious intentions; yet there is no anger or quarrelsomeness in her manner of handling of it, as we see in the way in which she represents General Tilney—the General is primarily an object of laughter. One feels that Jane Austen was constitutionally allergic to tyranny, but, if so, in this book she never openly attacks it or bitterly resents it. Such pugnacity and irascibility are in fact the basic constituents of tyranny, and the characteristics as well of the General, who casts Catherine out of the Abbey in a fit of unreasonable rage. Compared with him, Catherine is gentle in nature; she is a member of a family who are 'far from being an irritable race' (233). Yet even she is sometimes roused to anger. She harbours 'virtuous indignation' against the General, who she suspects has been a cruel husband (181). And later, in her own mild way, she expresses her indignation against the inconstant and mercenary Isabella and the flirtatious Captain Tilney; but Henry Tilney adroitly takes the edge off her indignation. Jane. Austen knew that 'virtuous indignation' was a dangerous thing. When one is driven by this emotion to denounce tyranny bitterly, the denunciation in turn can become tyranny, as the course of events in France in the 1790s, and the English reaction to it, well illustrate. Fully aware of this, Jane Austen refrained from outright hostile criticism of tyranny and, with characteristic humour, portrayed General Tilney as an object of laughter.

CHAPTER 2

Marianne and Mary:
Sense and Sensibility

In the opening scene in Molière's *Le Misanthrope*, Alceste, the great predecessor of Marianne Dashwood, severely accuses Philinte of insincere servility. In society he sees 'nothing but base flattery, injustice, selfishness, treachery, villainy',[1] and his friend's prudent observance of outward forms of civility in dealing with worthless people exasperates him. Like Marianne, he hates to 'conceal [his] feelings under a mask of vain compliment' and can never bring himself to say a single word that he does not really mean.[2] Perhaps Alceste is more virulent and aggressive than Marianne in his hatred of the world, but the latter is as stubborn as the former in her refusal to conform to the normal social conventions. In the representation of these nonconformists both Molière and Jane Austen are concerned with the dilemma of an intelligent, honest, passionate, and rather naive person, and there is even a vague undercurrent of tragedy in their struggle. In the case of *Le Misanthrope*, however, criticism of society is by no means the dramatist's intention. Erich Auerbach points out that in Molière's comedies '[n]ot the slightest trace of politics, of social or economic criticism, or of an analysis of the political, social, and economic bases of life is to be found'. He continues to argue: 'Molière's criticism is entirely moralistic; that is to say, it accepts the prevailing structure of society, takes for granted its justification, permanence, and general validity, and castigates the excesses occurring within its limits as ridiculous'.[3] Now we are going to ask how is the case with Jane Austen: does she also accept the current system of society and disapprove of Marianne's excessive behaviour as deviation from the social norms, or is she in any way inclined to criticize the society which drives Marianne to excesses? The question is worth asking, since the recent feminist criticism, with its shrewd penetration into the underlayer of the text, has called into question the traditional view of the novelist as a supporter of the established society. Of all Jane Austen's novels *Sense and Sensibility* is apparently most 'didactic', and feminist criticism is characteristically quite sceptical about what is apparent; but to solve our problem we cannot overlook the novel's overt message. Apart from the question of who is the true heroine, Elinor or Marianne, in *Sense and Sensibility* Jane Austen certainly wanted to depict Marianne the nonconformist, and we should attend to what the author says about her struggle.

Marianne is a girl of sensibility, and her sensibility makes her quite fastidious and even 'misanthropic'. In the sullen Mr Palmer Elinor perceives 'too great an aptitude to fancy himself as much superior to people in general, as he must feel himself to be to Mrs. Jennings and Charlotte' (304), and similar 'aptitude' is also found in Marianne. Being 'sensible and clever' herself (6), she too shows undisguised contempt for people in general. 'Marianne', the narrator comments, 'with excellent abilities and an excellent disposition, was neither reasonable nor candid. She expected from other people the same opinions and feelings as her own' (201–02). But in society she seldom finds persons who can satisfy her expectations, and she has 'never much toleration for any thing like impertinence, vulgarity, inferiority of parts, or even difference of taste from herself' (127). This contempt for people leads to contempt for social conventions. Her inattention to social forms is indeed repeatedly stressed, but hers is not from mere impatience of restraint; rather, it proceeds from her disdain for those practices. Obviously in her mind the rules of propriety generally observed in society are inevitably associated with the mediocre people she despises. For her to restrain one's feelings for propriety's sake is 'a disgraceful subjection of reason to common-place and mistaken notions' (53); that is, she regards the observance of the conventional mores of society as a servile surrender to foolish neighbours. So, in place of those outer guides of conduct, she has recourse to an inner guide: her own feelings. When Elinor admonishes her that 'the pleasantness of an employment does not always evince its propriety', Marianne retorts: 'On the contrary, nothing can be a stronger proof of it, Elinor; for if there had been any real impropriety in what I did, I should have been sensible of it at the time; for we always know when we are acting wrong, and with such a conviction I could have had no pleasure' (68). Her confidence in *the inner guide* is indeed very strong, yet this mode of behaviour is to be proved to have serious drawbacks. Elinor remarks to Colonel Brandon that Marianne's 'systems have all the unfortunate tendency of setting propriety at nought' (56), and why it is 'unfortunate' is one of the main issues of the novel.

What is naturally expected from the disregard of social forms may be confusion of society. Tony Tanner remarks that Jane Austen 'knew that a world in which everyone was totally sincere, telling always the truth for the sake of their own feelings and never any lies for the feelings of others, would be simply an anarchy, everybody's personal "form" cancelling out everybody else's'.[4] No doubt Jane Austen knew this; in *Mansfield Park* she describes the anarchic confusion resulting from the neglect of forms in the episode of the theatricals. But in this novel no great disturbance arises in spite of Marianne's habitual disregard of forms, and the main reason for this is Elinor's covering up.[5] Quite frequently we witness scenes in which Elinor tries to conceal or gloss over her sister's unconventionality or rudeness: 'and Elinor, to screen Marianne from particularity' (86); 'said Elinor, endeavouring to smooth away the offence' (145); 'To atone for this conduct therefore, Elinor took immediate possession of the post of civility which she had assigned herself' (160), and so on. Indeed, it is not difficult to imagine that, if it were not for Elinor, Marianne's conduct would occasion serious troubles wherever she went, but this potential evil attending her refusal to conform to social forms entirely escapes Marianne's notice.

Marianne's daring conduct also exposes her to the danger of bringing disgrace upon her own head. She openly displays her affection for Willoughby in Barton and later in London repeatedly writes letters to him; at the same time she is curiously reticent about the terms on which they stand with each other, and this worries Elinor much. She fears, though she does not articulate it, that if they were not engaged and Willoughby should prove unfaithful, her sister's conduct which evidently goes beyond the boundary prescribed by social convention would incur serious damage to her reputation. Actually they have not been engaged and Willoughby does desert Marianne; but fortunately Elinor's fear is not realized, for, far from censuring Marianne, her friends, who never suspect that they have *not* been engaged, are all inclined to sympathize with her in her grief while blaming Willoughby for his more glaring misconduct. That Elinor's apprehension has not been groundless, however, is shown by the story of the two Elizas. Without mentioning the miserable life and death of the 'disgraced' mother (208), the fate of the daughter alone would suffice to suggest what fatal consequences might result from a woman's indulging in affection without reference to social convention. Born as an offspring of her mother's 'guilty connection' (208), Eliza the daughter has been hidden from polite circles, and now her banishment from society is completed; Colonel Brandon is obliged, significantly, to '[remove] her and her child into the country' (211)—they are destined to live an obscure life. We shall return to this vulnerability of women later; but here we must note that the author, though carefully avoiding involving Marianne in such a fate, deliberately suggests that it might possibly have fallen on her.

But if she narrowly escapes social punishment, Marianne cannot escape what is in a way more injurious: the destructive power of her own feelings. Marianne's unleashing of emotions often serves only to damage herself without effecting any amelioration of circumstances, as is seen in the episode of the dinner party at John Dashwood's. The party, just like society in general, consists of many blunt-witted persons, no one quite interesting, the conversation extremely dull, though civilly conducted. Then Elinor's screen paintings happen to draw their attention, and Mrs Ferrars and Fanny Dashwood, who would miss no opportunity to mortify Elinor, praise the skill of Miss Morton, Edward's bride elect, at the expense of Elinor's work. Elinor herself would have borne this spiteful insinuation without betraying emotion, but Marianne cannot stand such an insult to her sister. No sense of decorum prevents her from making a sharp protest, which merely incurs anger from Mrs Ferrars and Fanny. Once let loose, her emotion cannot stop; in the end 'her spirits were quite overcome, and hiding her face on Elinor's shoulder, she burst into tears' (236). The party is of course spoiled, and though she recovers herself presently, 'her spirits retained the impression of what had passed, the whole evening' (236). Her just indignation certainly evokes our sympathy as well as that of Colonel Brandon; but the explosion of feelings practically brings about nothing but exhaustion of her own spirit. Indeed, Marianne's ordeal is an ordeal by this consuming power of feelings untrammelled by the rules of behaviour.[6]

Throughout the book, Marianne's self-indulgent weakness is placed side by side with Elinor's 'exertion' and 'fortitude'. In the opening chapter the narrator tells us that Elinor's 'feelings were strong; but she knew how to govern them' (6). The control of feelings is of course to a large extent a matter of will; but in this novel Jane Austen demonstrates, through Elinor's 'exertion', that the rules of behaviour are indispensable to self-command. Elinor perceives foolishness, vulgarity, selfishness, or ill-nature as well as, or even better than, Marianne does, but this does not dispose her to refuse to conform to social mores; on the contrary, with a constant will for self-control, she usually consults the conventional rules of behaviour as a guide to it. It is the convention which governs unmarried women's behaviour towards the opposite sex that occupies Elinor's mind when she is first inclined to subdue her affection for Edward despite her conviction of their mutual regard; she is well aware that the prospect of their marriage is quite gloomy and to parade affection without social authorization is against propriety. The point at issue here is not the rigidity of such convention but the fact that by this way Elinor preserves the equilibrium of her mind. Even on less serious occasions her method of self-control is the same. When Edward visits Barton, she is irritated at his coldness; yet 'she avoided every appearance of resentment or displeasure, and treated him as she thought he ought to be treated from the family connection' (89). Here to restrain her vexation she has recourse to the forms of civility required at the scene of ordinary social intercourse among relatives. Similarly, when Elinor, Lucy, and Edward are thrown together at Mrs Jennings's house in London, Elinor 'would not be frightened from paying him those attentions which, as a friend and almost a relation, were his due, by the observant eyes of Lucy' (241); she lets the duty of civility overcome her embarrassment. Thus the rules of propriety serve at once as a guide and aid to self-control. When feelings grow so strong that mere willpower becomes inadequate to curb them, the sense of obligation to abide by the rules proves to be a valuable help. Elinor's respect for her promise of secrecy about the engagement between Lucy and Edward is a typical example. Considering Lucy's mean motive for taking Elinor into her confidence, the promise might hardly be worth keeping with such conscientious efforts as Elinor makes; but those very efforts keep her from falling victim to her own emotions. Later she tells Marianne: '*Then*, if I had not been bound to silence, perhaps nothing could have kept me entirely—not even what I owed to my dearest friends—from openly shewing that I was *very* unhappy' (264). Elinor knows that to restrain emotions is not to abate them, and very frequently is her observance of the rules of propriety accompanied with unpleasantness or pain; yet it in return enables her to keep a smooth relationship with neighbours and relatives, protects her from the danger of scandalizing society, and, above all else, helps her to preserve her mental equilibrium. Marianne, on the other hand, who believes in indulging in feelings and disdains following any worldly rule of behaviour, has neither will nor means for self-control. At Barton she would not allow her passion for Willoughby to be checked by any social convention, and in London she would not avail herself of any social form to suppress her grief at being deserted. Her violent emotions are left to take their own course, corroding both her mind and body, which results in the fatal illness. 'Had I died,—it would have been self-destruction' (345)—Marianne quite appositely reviews her conduct.

Yet Marianne's suffering requires further consideration. Her ardent love and acute sorrow is often seen only in terms of excessive sensibility, but there is more to it. Her fervid devotion to Willoughby is in a sense a rebound from her strong repugnance for the world; she seeks in him a compensation, as it were, for the disgusting society full of stupidity, vulgarity, and selfishness. As a compensation he must and needs to be perfect; consequently, the Willoughby she loves is not what he really is but what she wishes him to be. As Alistair Duckworth points out, he is 'to a large degree an invention of the imaginative mind'.[7] This is implied as early as in the scene of their second meeting:

> Encouraged by this to a further examination of his opinions, she proceeded to question him on the subject of books; her favourite authors were brought forward and dwelt upon with so rapturous a delight, that any young man of five and twenty must have been insensible indeed, not to become an immediate convert to the excellence of such works, however disregarded before. Their taste was strikingly alike. The same books, the same passages were idolized by each—or if any difference appeared, any objection arose, it lasted no longer than till the force of her arguments and the brightness of her eyes could be displayed. He acquiesced in all her decisions, caught all her enthusiasm.... (47)

Obviously Willoughby is only complying with Marianne, or rather, the girl's ardour and charms are making him comply with her. At the same time, Jane Austen subtly hints that the very ardour of Marianne makes her blind to this. 'Their taste was strikingly alike' is not so much a statement of the fact as an allusion to Marianne's feverish sentiment. Willoughby has his talents, but his are talents for role playing. Howard Babb's minute analysis of Willoughby's speech teaches us that his feelings are not spontaneous ones, like those of Marianne's, but deliberately created ones— 'a work of art'.[8] Later Willoughby confesses to Elinor: 'I endeavoured, by every means in my power, to make myself pleasing to her' (320). In other occasions such simulation would not escape Marianne; yet her insight fails her—the urgent necessity of a compensation occasions it. Without the slightest consciousness of this, she gives herself up to an illusion— an illusion which is for her the only hope to live in the intolerable society. Willoughby's treachery, therefore, gives her a severer shock than that of mere love betrayed. When his unfaithfulness first bursts upon her, she typically chooses to blame the world:

> I could rather believe every creature of my acquaintance leagued together to ruin me in his opinion, than believe his nature capable of such cruelty.... Beyond you three [Elinor, Mrs Dashwood, and Edward], is there a creature in the world whom I would not rather

suspect of evil than Willoughby . . . ? (189)

But this desperate endeavour to acquit him is unavailing; before long the revelation of Eliza's story obliges her to admit his worthlessness. Her hope as well as her self-respect is sadly and irrevocably crushed.

Marianne's tragedy, then, is a tragedy of excessive animosity towards the world. While her disgust with people in general makes her reject the conventional rules of behaviour, it generates in her a blind passion for a worthless object, and as a result of this unfortunate combination her unrestrained emotions consume her spirit and strength. She cannot be cured of her affliction, therefore, unless her indiscriminate dissatisfaction with people which is the fundamental cause of it is removed. In the description of Marianne's grief Jane Austen tactfully inserts instances of the girl's arbitrary repulsion towards her acquaintances, such as her denial of Mrs Jennings's compassionate heart; these are reminders of her disease. Yet the illness at Cleveland brings her at last to realize the excess of her antipathy. After they return to Barton, Marianne penitently admits to Elinor her past injustice to her acquaintances; this is indeed the most moving scene of the book. To the reader who has ached for her gloomy struggle, it is a great relief to see 'her new character of candour' (372).

❦

Let us now turn our attention from Marianne's tribulation to the problem of Jane Austen's attitude towards her society. As we have seen, in this novel the advisability of conforming to the conventional rules of propriety is stressed, with the disadvantages attending their disregard implied or demonstrated. It does not necessarily follow, however, that Jane Austen was a supporter of the society of her time; there are some other points to be considered. It may be helpful here to refer to Auerbach's discussion of Molière's comedies again. He argues that Molière's 'realism, insofar as it has a serious and problematic side, is limited to the psychological and moral realm'.[9] If we confine our attention to the protagonists' activities, this argument can also be applied to Jane Austen. As is the case with

Alceste, Marianne's aversion to the world springs solely from her disgust with individuals and has nothing to do with the system of society; she refuses to follow social conventions, not because she sees any injustice in them, but because she equates them with the inferior people she despises. With Elinor the case is similar; we frequently hear her analyse the defects of people, but never hear her discuss those of society. As far as the sisters' dramas are concerned, they are certainly limited to the psychological and moral realm. But when we turn our eyes to the background, something different comes into view. Molière, Auerbach points out, 'consistently avoids any realistic concretizing, or even any penetrating criticism, of the political and economic aspects of the milieu in which his characters move'.[10] But this does not apply to Jane Austen; apart from politics, the novelist quite accurately represents the social and economic facts of life in those days, and sometimes her representation has a subtle shade of criticism. Mrs Dashwood, for example, is obliged to move from Norland to poor circumstances; the estate is secured to John Dashwood to whom 'the succession to the Norland estate was not so really important as to his sisters' (3), and John, letting himself be persuaded by his wife, abandons any plan of pecuniary assistance to his step-mother's family. Although Mrs Dashwood and her daughters seem to attribute the decline of their fortune only to human greediness, all this implicitly points to the despotism of patriarchy which exploits its female members. And then there is the story of the two Elizas; the tragic story of the mother also discloses the tyranny of patriarchy, and the daughter's fate reminds us of the existence of double standards, for she is now an exile from society, whereas Willoughby apparently suffers no severe social punishment for his misconduct. One may find, if one is inclined to, other instances which denote women's vulnerability or corruption of patriarchy. Obviously Jane Austen was fully aware of the oppressed state of women; and, as is seen in the way in which she suggests the possibility of Marianne's ruin through the story of the two Elizas, she consciously encircles the main action of the novel with the vague implications of the injustice of patriarchy. But what is the meaning of this? How should one reconcile such implications to her pointed advice to conform to social conventions?

For the clarification of the matter it may be useful to examine briefly the views of those critics who point out the implied grim realities we have just mentioned. Claudia L. Johnson regards the novel as an uncompromising criticism of the patriarchal society; carrying out an extensive research into the political and feminist controversy of the time, she argues that nearly all the evils of the patriarchal system that the contemporary progressive social criticism exposed are visualized in *Sense and Sensibility*.[11] LeRoy Smith, on the other hand, does not regard the implied social injustice as an accusation; he rather considers that the novel deals with the problem of woman's survival in an oppressive environment.[12] Their views present a contrast, but on the whole they are a little too much preoccupied with the vague social realities which encircle the main action; Johnson entirely overlooks, and Smith pays only partial attention to, the author's overt message, and they rather forcibly conjoin and adjust the heroines' dramas to that misty region of reality. There certainly is a gulf, however, between the main action and the encircling realm of opaque reality, and the only critic who perceives this gulf is Mary Poovey.[13] Drawing our attention to the grim realities of society presented in this novel, Poovey stresses the fact that they are only implied and not fully analysed. The novel's theme, she considers, is the control of the anarchic power of feelings with Christian moral principles, but the author fails to establish a reliable moral authority to justify the theme. One of the factors of this failure Poovey finds in that halfway attitude of the author. She analyses thus: Jane Austen employs realistic setting to enforce the necessity of controlling the romantic desire of Marianne, but if she goes so far into this realistic setting as exposes the defects of society, the very basis of the moral norms requisite to control feelings must necessarily be called into question; therefore she stops short in her realism and directs our eyes away from society to the self-indulgent individual. But, so Poovey would argue, the implicit criticism of patriarchy is enough to undermine the moral authority the author tries to establish. This argument is worth close attention, but it has its unsatisfactory elements. For one thing, Poovey's view of Marianne is a little too narrow. As our examination makes clear, what Jane Austen tries to hint at through Marianne's conduct is something more complicated than the mere danger of excessive feelings; the indulgence in feelings is only one aspect of her problem. For another thing, the standards of behaviour upheld in this novel need not be pinned down to the age in which it was written. Jane Austen of course uses the conventional rules of propriety of her time; yet when she stresses the necessity to follow rules, what she means by rules, it seems, is not so much the particular rules of her time as the rules in a more generalized sense. Is it to suggest this that she so carefully confines the main action within the strictly psychological and moral realm? Again, then, we are back to the question: what relation do the implied realities of society bear to the dramas of Elinor and Marianne?

Claudia Johnson tries to see in Marianne's conduct a shadow of such radical women intellectuals of those days as Mary Wollstonecraft or Mary Hays. Of course Mary Wollstonecraft as a feminist cannot be identified with Marianne who, as we have seen, has no consciousness of injustice with regard to the social system; nevertheless, some interesting parallels of behaviour pattern are certainly found between Marianne and Wollstonecraft, which are surely not a casual coincidence, and which, I think, throw light on our present problem. The first parallel is their 'principled determination to scorn the unworthy practices of the world', as Johnson puts it.[14] Needless to say, Wollstonecraft's disregard of social conventions was based on her disapproval of the patriarchal system that oppressed women. In his *Memoirs of the Author of The Rights of Woman* William Godwin testifies: 'she had through life trampled on those rules which are built on the assumption of the imbecility of her sex; and had trusted to the clearness of her spirit for the direction of her conduct, and to the integrity of her views for the vindication of her character'.[15] So, while rejecting social conventions, she, like Marianne, had full confidence in the inner guide. Although they differ in foundation, their principles of behaviour are indeed quite analogous. Not only 'those rules which are built on the assumption of the imbecility of her sex', Wollstonecraft also despised forms and ceremonies of everyday life. In her *Letters Written During a Short Residence in Sweden, Norway, and Denmark* (1796) she remarks:

> The Swedes pique themselves on their politeness; but far from

> being the polish of a cultivated mind, it consists merely of tiresome forms and ceremonies. So far indeed from entering immediately into your character, and making you feel instantly at your ease, like the well-bred French, their over-acted civility is a continual restraint on all your actions. The sort of superiority which a fortune gives when there is no superiority of education, excepting what consists in the observance of senseless forms, has a contrary effect than what is intended. . . .[16]

Clearly Wollstonecraft shared Marianne's contempt for the illiterate, and, like her, equated forms and ceremonies with the empty-headedness of those people. Indeed, the above passage reminds us of Marianne's piqued retort to Elinor's mild banter at her too familiar conversation with Willoughby, in which she describes an observer of forms as 'reserved, spiritless, dull, and deceitful', as opposed to being 'open and sincere' (48). Wollstonecraft and Marianne, except for the former's ardent critical spirit against patriarchy, show striking similarities in their unfettered conduct on their own principles. At the same time, that exception is worth particular notice.

The second parallel is their urge to seek for compensations. From her early years Wollstonecraft did not have many reasons to love the world she lived in, and her warm friendship with Fanny Blood in her youth might be seen in terms of compensation. Although her adolescent fervent adoration for this friend seems to have cooled down before long, she showed self-forgetful devotion to her till her death in 1785. But it is her tragic love affair with Gilbert Imlay that most attracts our notice. Her antipathy towards the world was no doubt accelerated after she came fully to realize women's subjugated situation in society; at the same time, she was extremely thirsty for love. In 1792 she published *A Vindication of the Rights of Woman* and cherished an unsatisfied affection for Fuseli; within this year she left England for France. About her mental state at this period Godwin writes: 'She felt herself alone, as it were, in the great mass of her species; and she repined when she reflected, that the best years of her life were spent in this comfortless solitude'.[17] In such a state of unfulfilled loneliness she met Imlay in France in 1793; she fell in love with him, married him, and bore his child. But her happiness did not last long; in the following year he deserted her. Yet she could not give him up, and till the final separation with him in 1796, her lingering affection and his heartless response caused her to experience severest agonies, including the two attempts at suicide. Imlay seems to have had certain talents and an attractive personality, but evidently he was too fickle and faithless to be a worthy object of her ardent devotion—so much so that one is rather surprised to see how blind she was at first and how reluctant she was to give him up later. Claire Tomalin observes thus:

> Once she began to fall in love, she constructed a mental image of him which bore little relation to his true character. In her very last letters to him she refers to this image, clinging to it as some sort of justification for having involved herself with him in the first place, and probably Imlay too for a while imagined himself into the flattering new role in which he could perform to a new audience.[18]

Indeed, this illusory affection bears remarkable resemblance to that of Marianne. Of course, Wollstonecraft's unfortunate infatuation with Imlay may not be attributed to her enmity to society alone; but it was certainly a chief factor in it. Like Marianne, she sought a compensation for the dissatisfactory world in a worthless man—a libertine in disguise; and just as 'Marianne could never love by halves' (379), so 'a heart like hers was not formed to nourish affection by halves',[19] however unworthy the object of that affection might be. Furthermore, she, like Marianne, had no guide and help in the conventional rules of propriety to check her emotions. The result of all this was her desperate attempts at self-destruction.

The history of the composition of *Sense and Sensibility* is a little complicated and not clearly known, but it seems certain that Jane Austen began it in the narrative form in November 1797, less than three months after the death of Wollstonecraft.[20] Before the appearance of Godwin's *Memoirs* in 1798 which caused a great scandal, the name of Mary Wollstonecraft and her works were by no means abhorred or shunned by the public. Although somewhat notorious, *A Vindication*, so Tomalin says, 'was reviewed in respectful tones and circulated merrily all over the British Isles'.[21] Tomalin also suggests the probability of Jane Austen's knowledge of Mary's pathetic story, informing us of a link between them,[22] and those parallels we have just examined between Marianne and Wollstonecraft seem to leave little room to doubt the novelist's familiarity with the latter's life story as well as such of her works as *A Vindication* and *A Short Residence* (and perhaps even *Memoirs*, too). If so, however, it is not that Jane Austen attempted to reproduce Wollstonecraft's life in Marianne; rather, she extracted from Wollstonecraft's life story the basic behaviour pattern of a person who was opposed to society and fleshed it out anew into the character of Marianne. In this operation her discernment is quite acute and her skill incomparable. But why then did she so thoroughly exclude the element of social criticism from Marianne's hatred of the world? and how is this exclusion related to her vague representation of the grim realities of the society of her age?

It is worth remembering here Jane Austen's general method of novel writing. As Chapman points out, one of the features of her composition is her scrupulous respect for exactness in details.[23] Her stories and characters are of course fictional, but she was remarkably attentive to accuracy in the framework of her fiction, such as topography, dates, and manners. It appears that she abandoned the use of hedgerows in *Mansfield Park* because Northamptonshire was not a country of hedgerows. When she decided to publish *Northanger Abbey* more than ten years after it was composed, she took the trouble to put the 'Advertisement' to the novel in which she suggested the changes of places or manners that had occurred during that period. Of course such factualism does not necessarily mean that Jane Austen merely tried to mirror the particular mode of life of her age; it rather indicates her concern for verisimilitude, and she was well aware that verisimilitude was essential to the object of her art—the presentation of the truth of life. This bears close relation to another feature of her composition: the economy of description. In her comments on the novels of her niece Anna, she remarks: 'your descriptions are often more minute than will be liked. You give too many particulars of right hand & left'.[24]

And in her own works she generally refrains from giving this kind of detail. We are informed very little, for example, of the room arrangement of Mansfield Park or of the personal appearance of Fanny Price, though we have little doubt that the author envisaged every detail about them. But if we are left in the dark concerning these concrete aspects, we cannot fail to have definite notions about more essential points, such as the atmosphere of Mansfield Park or the character of Fanny. Jane Austen paid close attention to accuracy in the framework of her fiction for the sake of verisimilitude, but once that verisimilitude attained, she made no further reference to details, for her aim was not to reconstruct the life of her age but to extract the essence of life from it.

The world of Jane Austen's novels, then, is at once closely linked to and independent of her age, and in considering *Sense and Sensibility* we should especially bear this in mind. As we have seen, what the author tries to emphasize in this novel is the danger of self-ruin that accompanies a defiant attitude towards society, and this is what the Dashwood sisters' dramas are concerned with. Obviously Jane Austen was roused to deal with this theme by the living examples found in her contemporary society—particularly by that of Mary Wollstonecraft. From Marianne's aversion to the world, however, the novelist carefully excluded the element of the indignation at social injustice which in Wollstonecraft's case was the chief motive for her rejection of the established conventions; instead, she based Marianne's antipathy towards society on her disgust with human imperfections—such as foolishness, vulgarity, or selfishness—which were not to be tied to any particular period or society. Jane Austen was no doubt well aware of the defects of her society which Wollstonecraft attacked, but what she wished to treat in this novel is not the problem of social injustice; she did not wish the essential drama of the book entangled in the diseases peculiar to her age—she wished, in short, to detach it from the contemporary society. The rules of behaviour she used were certainly those of her age, and her description of them is quite faithful; yet this was rather for the sake of verisimilitude than for endorsing the moral code of her society. Since the cause of Marianne's antipathy towards society is something independent of her age, it is just possible to see its effects in the same point of view; that is, the rules of propriety which she disregards (and which Elinor follows) need not be seen as the particular rules of this age; rather, they should be seen as rules in a general sense. If seen as such, Marianne's self-destructive struggle, just like the case with Alceste, comes to have a timeless nature; as long as society exists, this can happen in any age and under any social circumstances.

One could say that in *Sense and Sensibility* Jane Austen attempted to give an indirect answer to the question which the progressive social criticism of her day put forward. Mary Wollstonecraft and other radical intellectuals called into question the current system of society which oppressed women; they asked, as it were, whether it was just or not. To this Jane Austen provided no direct answer; at least she could not say that it was just, for she knew that it was not. On the other hand she also forbore to disapprove of her society, for she knew that the disapprobation of its system must necessarily lead to the denial of the whole social convention; she rather perceived the peril attending such a rebellious attitude, and, indeed, Wollstonecraft's tragic life story well illustrated this. Perhaps Jane Austen was not exactly a conservative, but, no matter how unfair and oppressive the society might be to women, she judged it wiser and safer to abide by its laws and customs than to act in defiance of them. When she tried to express this view in the novel, however, she was confronted with the difficult problem of satisfying two demands at once: namely, to demonstrate the risks involved in anti-social behaviour, and to avoid discussing the rights or wrongs of patriarchy. If, as Mary Poovey's argument suggests, Marianne's dissatisfaction were directed to the system of society, and this dissatisfaction were justifiable (which would be inevitable), then her disregard of the conventional rules of propriety which are grounded on that doubtful social system would also become justifiable; in that case the novel's theme would collapse. The novelist, therefore, left Marianne unaware of the injustice of the patriarchal order; instead, she placed such a stupid or unpleasant set of people round this sensitive heroine as would induce her to feel disgusted with society. Thus Jane Austen succeeded in detaching Marianne's struggle from the contemporary social context and demonstrating the disadvantages which accompanied the Wollstonecraftian defiant conduct. A natural question here arises: why then did she have to take the trouble to hint so elaborately at the gloomy realities of her society? When we consider that those episodes which suggest the tyranny and corruption of patriarchy, such as the casting out of the Dashwood family from Norland or the story of the two Elizas, are so interwoven as not to influence the dramas of Elinor and Marianne, and yet on the whole they serve to remind us of the nature of the society in which they live, we might say that her seemingly unnecessary halfway realism is a device to intimate to the reader that the novel is an oblique comment on the radical social criticism of her time. This subtle art is a reminder, so to speak, of the author's motive for writing the novel. It might also be said that the ruin of Marianne's character implied through the tale of the Elizas, together with Elinor's silent concern for her reputation, is a distant allusion to the posthumous infamy that fell on Wollstonecraft; the melancholy tone of that tale perhaps indicates Jane Austen's pity for that woman who was hapless even after her death.

Jane Austen's attitude was in a sense evasive; and yet no one can deny that a profound insight into the relationship between the individual and society pervades the whole of *Sense and Sensibility*. Mary Wollstonecraft might have believed that society would become flawless if only her ideals could be realized; but Jane Austen knew that any society could not be so perfect, and she would rather choose to try her best in the society in which she happened to live than to reject and rebel against it. However negative it may appear to some, this was her philosophy of life, and it may account for the joy given to novel readers through the changing fashion of ages.

CHAPTER 3

Too Much Antipathy towards Too Much Formality:
Pride and Prejudice

The figure of a young girl who stands aloof from the surrounding people is familiar in Jane Austen's novels. Whether it is the state she herself voluntarily seeks—as with Marianne Dashwood—or the state to which she is helplessly abandoned—as with Fanny Price—this estrangement usually involves a certain material disparity in value judgements between her and other people, and the struggle to overcome this gulf is what she has to go through to achieve maturity. And so is the case of Elizabeth Bennet, the heroine of *Pride and Prejudice*.

At first glance, this 'delightful . . . creature', as the author herself calls her,[1] seems to suggest nothing of solitariness or isolation, and certainly she does not follow Marianne by removing herself in an ostentatious manner from those around her and withdrawing into stubborn silence and secrecy. Yet Elizabeth is in fact as much mentally estranged from the surrounding people as Marianne, and if silence and secrecy are the manifestations of Marianne's estrangement, it is laughter that denotes that of Elizabeth. Laughter is indeed inseparable from our image of this 'delightful' heroine, who herself openly declares, 'I dearly love a laugh' (57). With 'a lively, playful disposition' which delights in 'any thing ridiculous', she chooses to laugh even at Darcy's arrogant rudeness in the memorable scene of the Meryton ball (12). But her laughter, ever ready to catch at 'any thing ridiculous', is by no means a mere manifestation of cheerfulness or good humour; with all her playfulness, her mirth directed at human folly contains something very poignant in it.[2] Actually, Elizabeth's laughter is a form of keen antipathy, and the fact that she is continually laughing—

that is, she continually perceives absurdity—is certainly indicative of her mental isolation from the society to which she belongs.

This detachment of Elizabeth is very important, and to grasp the full meaning of it, we need to look closely at the society described in this novel which she finds full of absurdities—we shall return to her solitary struggle later. In the opening chapter of the book, Mrs Bennet complains to her husband that he would not pay a courtesy visit to a newcomer at Netherfield Park; it will be impossible, says she, for her or her daughters to visit him, if Mr Bennet does not. This impossibility arises from the convention of the time that forbade women's initiative in social intercourse, and such minutely prescribed rules of propriety are indeed dominant in the novel's world. Later in the book there is a scene where Lydia, who has returned home as Mrs Wickham, walks up to her eldest sister as the family go to the dining parlour and says: 'Ah! Jane, I take your place now, and you must go lower, because I am a married woman' (317). What Lydia refers to here is the order of precedence, according to which the family enter the dining room—usually the father and mother first, and then the daughters in order of birth. But now Lydia claims her right as a married woman, who takes precedence over a single one. As David M. Shapard comments, 'Lydia's statement suggests that the Bennets follow rules of precedence as a matter of course, even for purely family dinners, a practice that reveals the formality prevailing in this society'.[3]

Of course any society has its own rules; without them society simply cannot exist. Nor is the degree of formality shown in those scenes by any means peculiar to the novel; at the outset of *Persuasion* the narrator tells us that for thirteen years Elizabeth, as the eldest daughter of Sir Walter Elliot, had been 'leading the way to the chaise and four, and walking immediately after Lady Russell out of all the drawing-rooms and dining-rooms in the country' (*P* 7).[4] But what is conspicuous in *Pride and Prejudice* is that these rules are respected with rather too much rigidity. In the early part of the book there is an episode in which Elizabeth takes a long solitary walk through muddy fields to Netherfield Park in order to attend to her sick sister Jane, and the reactions of the surrounding people are a good illustration of the inflexibility. Her mother protests against her attempt, saying: 'You will not be fit to be seen when you get there'. Her pedantic sister Mary remarks that 'exertion should always be in proportion to what is required' (32). Darcy's sentiment echoes Mary's words; he feels 'doubt as to the occasion's justifying her coming so far alone' (33). Above all the rest, the most merciless are Miss Bingley and Mrs Hurst; they show a contemptuous surprise at the young girl's lonely country walk, and are aghast at her dirty appearance which results from it. The former concludes: 'It seems to me to shew an abominable sort of conceited independence, a most country town indifference to decorum' (36). The action of Elizabeth is certainly bold, but the emergency and her sisterly affection may amply justify its slight deviation from conventional propriety. Yet no such concessions are to be granted—this is the principle of the society portrayed in this novel.[5]

The rules of propriety are important as a lubricant of social intercourse, but the people in the book tend to forget this; or, rather, they tend to attach much more significance to them than their original function would justify, and this kind of undue or inflexible adherence to social forms is comically exaggerated in certain characters. Sir William Lucas is a man who '[occupies] himself solely in being civil to all the world' (18), and whose civilities [are] worn out' (152); for him the forms of civility are things which are merely to be mechanically repeated. But the character who is most memorable in his apish adherence to forms is Mr Collins. His ceremonious politeness is always extravagant, and his endless thanks and apologies are especially ludicrous. He is totally oblivious to the original purpose of these forms, and we can see how his over-adherence to forms becomes an impediment to smooth social intercourse in the scene where he receives Elizabeth and the Lucases to the Hansford Parsonage:

> She [Elizabeth] saw instantly that her cousin's manners were not altered by his marriage; his formal civility was just what it had been, and he detained her some minutes at the gate to hear and satisfy his enquiries after all her family. They were then, with no other delay than his pointing out the neatness of the entrance, taken into the house; and as soon as they were in the parlour, he welcomed them

a second time with ostentatious formality to his humble abode, and punctually repeated all his wife's offers of refreshment. (155)

In contrast to this clumsy work, later when they are invited to dinner at Rosings Park, the office of introduction is assigned to Mrs Collins, instead of her husband, so that the ceremony is 'performed in a proper manner, without any of those apologies and thanks which he would have thought necessary' (161).

Mr Collins is indeed a comical representative of the novel's world in which the conventional rules of behaviour are so minute and so rigidly stuck to as to impede and oppress man's natural activities. In parallel with this over-adherence to rules of behaviour, another feature that is also dominant in the novel is the over-adherence to rank. It might be natural that in a society in which a hierarchy is firmly established those in higher positions should sometimes become pompous and imperative, but in this novel adherence to rank of such characters as Darcy and Lady Catherine de Bourgh—especially their overweening arrogance towards social inferiors—seems to be deliberately emphasized. Darcy is, as soon as he appears in the book, stamped as insufferably proud; he considers it a disgrace to behave affably in such vulgar assemblies as the Meryton ball, and does not deign to conceal his lofty contempt. He obviously assumes his high social position is a mark of 'superiority of mind' (57), and refuses to be on familiar terms with his inferiors. Similarly, or more extremely, haughty is his aunt Lady Catherine (indeed, Lady Catherine is a bold caricature of Darcy, as Mrs Norris is of Sir Thomas Bertram, or Mrs Elton is of Emma). On the reception of Elizabeth and the Lucases at Rosings Park, '[h]er air was not conciliating, nor was her manner of receiving them, such as to make her visitors forget their inferior rank' (162). She cannot for a moment bear the idea that she should be connected with attorneys or tradesmen, and Pemberley—her nephew's estate—would be 'polluted' (357), she declares, if it should receive visitors 'from the city' (388). It is not, though, that Darcy and Lady Catherine are negligent of the responsibility which their status assigns to them; on the contrary, Darcy 'is the best landlord, and the best master . . . that ever lived', as Mrs Reynolds describes him (249), and Lady Catherine, though 'not in the commission of the peace for the county', is 'a most active magistrate in her own parish' (169). But their problem is that they put much more emphasis on and attach much more meaning to rank than is necessary or rational, a manifestation of which is their undue hauteur.

One notes, however, that in the novel's world such attitude of the gentry is received very compliantly. When Darcy behaves haughtily at the Meryton ball, we are told that everybody is offended; but, in fact, apart from the capricious Mrs Bennet, it is Elizabeth alone who is really offended at his manners. The others' views are represented in Charlotte Lucas's words:

> 'His pride . . . does not offend *me* so much as pride often does, because there is an excuse for it. One cannot wonder that so very fine a young man, with family, fortune, every thing in his favour, should think highly of himself. If I may so express it, he has a *right* to be proud.' (20)

Darcy's pride sometimes leads him to commit even injurious acts, such as his severing of Bingley from Jane. In his letter to Elizabeth he asserts that he did it in order to save his friend from an imprudent match. But this was by no means the one and only motive. There had been a plan of union between his sister and Bingley, and the narrator observes: 'without meaning that it should affect his endeavour to separate him from Miss Bennet, it is probable that it might add something to his lively concern for the welfare of his friend' (270). What is insinuated in the delicate phraseology is that Darcy's motives in the action were not quite as disinterested as he avows, and we may discern yet another strong impetus at work in the matter. It is essentially his conceited belief in his own superiority that drives him to dictate to Bingley. His exertion, that is, is really not so much for Bingley's sake as for the gratification of his own self-esteem. Elizabeth, who instinctively detects this, expresses to Colonel Fitzwilliam her unfeigned disapprobation:

> 'I do not see what right Mr. Darcy had to decide on the propriety

of his friend's inclination, or why, upon his own judgment alone, he was to determine and direct in what manner that friend was to be happy.' (185–86)

Indeed, the eventual happy reunion of Jane and Bingley proves that it is no more than a very officious interference. Yet no one perceives the unjustness of this arbitrary directorship except Elizabeth. In the case of Lady Catherine, this dictatorial tendency is more flagrant: 'nothing was beneath this great Lady's attention, which could furnish her with an occasion of dictating to others' (163). And, as in Darcy's case, her instructions are often very officious; but she is 'not used to have her judgment controverted' (163), and the obsequious Mr Collins at its head, everybody is compliant with her except, again, Elizabeth.

We can say, then, that in the novel's world society in general over-adheres to rank, just as it over-adheres to the rules of behaviour, with most of the restrictions and inconveniences which are caused by it quite readily tolerated. And the spirit of such society is most clearly embodied in the people's attitude towards marriage. Marriage in those days, and especially among the upper classes, was certainly not only a matter of mutual affection, but also an important institution on which depended continuation of families. Yet in the world of the novel the case is extreme; the people so stick to birth and rank that it is rather a matter of course that marriages are made for interests or convenience, without any regard to the feelings of the parties concerned. Thus Darcy, who has been conditioned by this climate, finds it 'due to the consequence he [is] wounding' to convince Elizabeth that it is an exceptional condescension that he should offer his hand to a social inferior such as her (189). Later, when these two are finally united after many vicissitudes, Lady Catherine tries to break up their marriage in order to accomplish the 'planned' union between Darcy and her own daughter (355)—a union purely based on the family interests. One may notice that such attitudes towards marriage are again comically exaggerated in Mr Collins. He is to marry Charlotte Lucas eventually, but he first attempts to choose his wife from among the five Miss Bennets as 'atonement' (70), as he is to inherit their father's estate on account of the entailed interest he possesses. And according to 'his strictest notions of what was due to seniority' (70), he selects first Jane, then Elizabeth (though his intention is frustrated in both cases). This impersonal selection of a wife, dictated indeed by rules of precedence, is symbolic of the prevailing atmosphere in the novel's world which gives priority to claims of society over any other.

Having examined the peculiar features of the society described in the novel, we might at this point survey the social situation from the late eighteenth to the early nineteenth century, during which the novel was composed, in order to see how these features are linked to the actual society of the times. Generally speaking, English people in the eighteenth century were notorious for their easy-going indifference to manners and morals; but their tastes and behaviour began to change gradually during the second half of the century, and, as many historians demonstrate, from the 1780s onward—especially after the outbreak of the French Revolution—England experienced a most thorough reformation of manners and morals.[6] The 1780s was marked by the appearance of various movements for moral reform, and, among the rest, the most energetic and influential were the activities of the Evangelicals, who eagerly joined in any scheme to further reformation of manners and revival of religion. In the next decade, these activities received an invaluable aid from the impact of the French Revolution. In the midst of the political agitation the general need for spiritual comfort brought many people to the church they had long abandoned, and the strict conservative policy which was adopted by the English authorities for fear of contagion of French liberalism produced an ideal soil for the reformation. Anti-Jacobinism was so widely and so successfully propagated as to make the people vigilant against any form of liberalism, including liberty of manners, and the Evangelical reformers made effective use of this climate to spread their teachings (sometimes they combined their teachings with political propaganda, such as Hannah More's *Cheap Repository Tracts* [1795–98]). Under these circumstances people became stricter and stricter on the matter of manners and morals. The shift in national character which had thus started in the 1790s was accelerated after the turn of the century, and by the time Prince George took the regency, a new outlook on life permeated the nation—very strict standards of conduct were now established. The over-formality in *Pride and Prejudice* is undoubtedly a reflection of this new-born inflexible society in the early nineteenth century.

As for the excessive fidelity to rank, one could associate it with the rigid conservatism of those days that was brought about by the strong reaction against the French Revolution. The ruling classes were very anxious to maintain the *status quo*, and the spirit of 'adherence to the old and tried', as Abraham Lincoln put it, was diffused throughout the country by their successful anti-liberalism propaganda. As a result, not only the landed elite but the people in general became more than ever mindful of the differentiation of status. But there was another context for the gentry's adherence to their position: the rapid growth of their inferiors.

Along with the political conservatism, what marked the period around the turn of the century was the remarkable progress of industry. As we have seen in Chapter 1, many landowners were quite willing to embrace this current and derived a substantial profit from it. At the same time, they were by no means warmly disposed towards those who were raising themselves in the new industrial era, and who began, if not to usurp, but at least to encroach on their own privileged territory. The gentry chose to turn their back to those parvenu classes, and in the early decades of the nineteenth century a gulf began to open between them and their inferiors. In *Pride and Prejudice* Darcy's proud detachment in the Meryton assembly suggests this new social atmosphere, and in his later confession that from his childhood he has been 'allowed, encouraged, almost taught . . . to care for none beyond [his] own family circle, to think meanly of all the rest of the world, to *wish* at least to think meanly of their sense and worth compared with [his] own' (369), we detect the uneasiness and defensiveness that were dominant emotions among the gentry in this period.

A natural question then arises concerning the relationship between Darcy and Bingley. The Bingleys 'were of a respectable family in the north of England', and their 'fortune . . . had been acquired by trade' (15). They are thus a typical *nouveau-riche* family of this period, and one wonders why Darcy should choose to cultivate 'a very steady friendship' with a man of this social standing. We don't know exactly how they became acquainted in the first place—presumably they met at one of social gatherings in London. As for the reasons for the intimacy they have developed since, we are left to gather from such succinct comments:

> Bingley was endeared to Darcy by the easiness, openness, ductility of his temper, though no disposition could offer a greater contrast to his own, and though with his own he never appeared dissatisfied. On the strength of Darcy's regard Bingley had the firmest reliance, and of his judgment the highest opinion. (16)

A key word in the passage may be 'ductility'. Darcy indeed loves 'having somebody at his disposal', as Elizabeth insinuates to Colonel Fitzwilliam (184), and when she hears an account from him of Darcy's exertion for 'a friend', she concludes this 'friend' to be none other than Bingley, since '[t]here could not exist in the world *two* men, over whom Mr. Darcy could have such boundless influence' (186). Thus Bingley, with all his fabulous fortune ('nearly an hundred thousand pounds'), could in no way be a menace to Darcy; on the contrary, his 'ductility' rather consolidates the latter's superior position. Indeed, he is to Darcy as Harriet Smith is to Emma Woodhouse, and Darcy's mentality there certainly bears some resemblance to that of Emma, who demonstratively befriends those who, like the Westons and Harriet, readily show their obedient respect for her, but is rather cold and haughty to those who, like the Coles and Jane Fairfax, keep a distance from her. As with the case of Emma, Darcy's officious patronage of a docile man speaks of a mind that is driven to show off his own powers and status.[7]

Pride and Prejudice was originally written during the years 1796–97 under the title of *First Impressions*, and the work is believed to have undergone considerable revision before its publication in 1813. In his edition R. W. Chapman demonstrated that the author used the calendar of 1811–12 for the action of the novel, and, if so, it would be most natural to assume that it was revised at this period.[8] Now that the original version is lost, we cannot know exactly how the author revised it; in spite of this complicated history of composition, however, there seems to be no obscurity as regards the time to which the fictional events belong, for, as we have seen, the social features depicted in the novel distinctly point to the time around 1810. Actually, the social conditions in the 1810s had much altered from those in the 1790s, and when Jane Austen settled in Chawton Cottage and resumed novel writing, many customs that had been prevailing in her youth had disappeared. We know that in her teens her family enjoyed amateur theatricals, but thanks to the severe attacks from the reformers, this innocent pastime was now seldom seen among decent people. This is of course only an instance, and so great were the changes in society that when in 1816 she intended the publication of *Northanger Abbey*, she felt obliged to add the 'Advertisement' to the novel, in which she entreats the reader to remember 'that thirteen years have passed since it was finished, many more since it was begun, and that during that period, places, manners, books, and opinions have undergone considerable changes'.[9] In preparing the publication of *Pride and Prejudice* during 1811–12, however, aware of the changes in society that had occurred since it was first written in the late 1790s, she extensively revised the work and deftly wove a criticism of the new social climate into it.

To probe the author's critical intention, let us now return to Elizabeth and her solitary struggle. With her seemingly progressive ideas, Elizabeth tends to be regarded as representing 'modern' personality; in fact, however, her character—her value judgements and modes of thought—is in many ways tied to the eighteenth century. As we have seen, Elizabeth is conspicuous for her witty satirical laughter, and wit and satire were indeed dominant features of eighteenth-century literature. She is often compared with such heroines of the Restoration comedies as Millamant in William Congreve's *The Way of the World* (1700),[10] and in her policy on laughter we can discern a sort of cultural tradition. There is an interesting exchange between her and Darcy at Netherfield Park about the subject of laughter. To Elizabeth who professes an intense passion for a laugh, Darcy insinuates that she may be indiscriminate in her derision. But she returns:

> 'I hope I never ridicule what is wise or good. Follies and nonsense, whims and inconsistencies *do* divert me, I own, and I laugh at them whenever I can' (57).

This principle of Elizabeth on laughter—that one should laugh only at what is ridiculous or absurd—reminds one of that of Henry Fielding formulated in the Preface to *Joseph Andrews*. In his discourse on 'the ridiculous' Fielding also differentiates what should be laughed at from what should not be. We cannot laugh, he argues, at a wretched family shivering with cold and languishing with hunger in a poor house; but 'should we discover there a Grate, instead of Coals, adorned with Flowers, empty Plate or China Dishes on the Side-board, or any other Affectation of Riches and Finery either on their Persons or in their Furniture; we might then indeed be excused, for ridiculing so fantastical an Appearance'.[11] In this Preface Fielding expounds the theory that the source of the true ridiculous is affectation arising from vanity and hypocrisy. In his later discussion on 'humour' in *The Covent-Garden Journal*, No. 55 (July 18, 1752), Fielding also includes 'excess' as another source of the ridiculous:

> Excess, says Horace, even in the Pursuit of Virtue, will lead a wise and good Man into Folly and Vice.—So will it subject him to Ridicule; for into this, says the judicious Abbé Bellegarde, a Man may tumble headlong with an excellent Understanding, and with the most laudable Qualities. Piety, Patriotism, Loyalty, Parental Affection, &c. have all afforded Characters of Humour for the Stage.[12]

As we have examined, the novel's world indeed abounds with instances of 'excess'—excess in attachment to social forms and systems—and Elizabeth who laughs at them could be seen as an inheritor of the true eighteenth-century comic spirit.

But this wittiness of Elizabeth reminiscent of the eighteenth century is on the whole incompatible with the new ethos of the nineteenth century. Hannah More, one of the leading Evangelicals of the day, started her career as a witty writer in the 1770s; but later she forsook her humour and devoted herself to serious moral writings. In *Strictures on the Modern System of Female Education* (1799) she severely denounces 'ridicule' as 'the most deadly weapon in the whole arsenal of impiety':

> An age which values itself on parody, burlesque, irony, and caricature, produces little that is sublime, either in genius or in virtue; but they *amuse*, and we live in an age which *must* be amused, though genius, feeling, truth, and principle, be the sacrifice. Nothing chills the ardours of devotion like a frigid sarcasm; and, in the season of youth, the mind should be kept particularly clear of all light associations.[13]

In this sober preaching (a prototype, one may say, of Mr Collins's 'lofty' morality) no vestige remains of 'the popular playwright, society "blue stocking", light-weight poet and wit of the early days',[14] and, indeed, this change in Hannah More is symbolic of the change of social character in this period; wit and satire came to be suppressed in the growing inclination for seriousness.

Another and perhaps less conspicuous aspect of Elizabeth that is associated with the eighteenth century is her balanced attitude, respecting the demands of both society and the individual equally. In his '*Pride and Prejudice* in the Eighteenth-Century Mode', Samuel Kliger argues that throughout the eighteenth century such parallel antitheses as art versus nature, reason versus feeling, and rules versus originality, were commonly employed in aesthetic and ethical debate, and the 'rationalistic temper of the period required that excellence be found in a mean between two extremes'.[15] The art-nature antithesis can be extended, as Kiger suggests, to the more general opposition between society and the individual, and the need for compromise and adjustment between the demands of both sides was emphasized in eighteenth-century society.

Kliger's argument which laid open the way the theme of the art-nature dialectic works in the novel has not lost its momentum today. Putting emphasis on the wide applicability of the theme, Keneth L. Moler observes:

> If we view *Pride and Prejudice* in the light of the art-nature antithesis and bear in mind the widespread use of this dialectic in political, aesthetic, and other sorts of intellectual discourse of the period, it becomes clear that Austen is dealing, in human terms, with the forces *behind* the revolutions of her day. The differences between Elizabeth and Darcy are the differences between Paine and Burke, between romantic and classic.[16]

Most of the recent critical debates, then, such as the 'conservative' versus 'subversive' dispute, contain nothing essentially new in them, but are merely the refashioning of Kliger's ground-breaking study. Yet there is one aspect of his argument—and that of many others who have followed him, including Moler—which is difficult to accept, namely that Elizabeth is stamped as a representative of only one pole of the art-nature antithesis. If she is absolutely on the side of 'nature' and antipathetic to all 'arts'— that is, all the man-made rules and systems—how does one account for her frequent efforts to conform herself to the rules of behaviour? When she is unexpectedly informed of Charlotte's engagement with Mr Collins, for example, she is so astonished 'as to overcome at first the bounds of decorum'; but soon recollecting herself, and 'making a strong effort for it, was able to assure her with tolerable firmness that . . . she wished her all imaginable happiness' (124–25). If she 'possesses the illusion of total freedom' and is 'contemptuous of all conventions that constrict the individual's freedom', as A. Walton Litz puts it,[17] why does she not in this scene go on venting her contemptuous surprise which is her natural emotion, instead of trying to suppress it in compliance with the rules of decorum? True, she sometimes breaks the rules of propriety intentionally, such as her walk to Netherfield; but on such occasions she has valid reasons, and she never infringes social conventions indiscriminately. She possesses the true eighteenth-century spirit of esteeming the happy mean, and the reason why she appears to be a conspicuous non-conformist is that those around her are all too strict in their conformity to the forms of society.

At one point Elizabeth complains to Jane: 'There are few people whom I really love, and still fewer of whom I think well. The more I see of the world, the more am I dissatisfied with it' (135). Being a child of the age of reason, she cannot conform herself to the new climate of society which puts such undue stress on forms—whether forms for social intercourse or forms for social organization—as to oppress individuality to the extreme, and so she fights a solitary battle with the irrationality that encompasses her, with her wit as a weapon. Her stance is indeed defiant: when she notices that Darcy's eyes are frequently fixed on her, she reasons thus:

> She could only imagine . . . that she drew his notice because there was a something about her more wrong and reprehensible, according to his ideas of right, than in any other person present. The supposition did not pain her. She liked him too little to care for his approbation. (51)

Darcy's 'ideas of right', as Elizabeth sees them, are little more than offspring of slavish compliance with the rules of propriety—an attitude which she has habitually laughed at as 'absurd' or 'ridiculous'. She therefore defies any judgement formed by such criteria. In a similar way she scorns the irrational sticking to rank which is prevalent around her. When she and the Lucases make their first appearance at Rosings Park, in contrast to the latter who stand in trembling awe of Lady Catherine, Elizabeth tries to dispel from herself any undue reverence for her:

> She had heard nothing of Lady Catherine that spoke her awful from any extraordinary talents or miraculous virtue, and the mere stateliness of money and rank, she thought she could witness without trepidation. (161)

And later in their conversation Elizabeth contends with Lady Catherine about a trivial matter, and is half proud of herself 'to be the first creature who had ever dared to trifle with' this great Lady (166). (It should be noted, however, that here too Elizabeth is by no means an indiscriminate infringer of the social code; when Lady Catherine pours officious 'instructions' upon her about her musical performance, 'Elizabeth received them with all the forbearance of civility' [176]—a piece of unobtrusive discretion in the midst of bold defiance.)

It may be natural that this defiant posture should invite criticism, and actually Elizabeth's manners are often condemned as 'impertinent' (she herself archly asks Darcy at the end of the book, 'did you admire me for my impertinence?' [380]). It is worth noting that she incurs the displeasure not only of the characters in the book but also of the contemporary reader. In her letter written in 1814 Mary Russell Mitford reviles at her thus:

> The want of elegance is almost the only want in Miss Austen. . . . it is impossible not to feel in every line of *Pride and Prejudice*, in every word of 'Elizabeth,' the entire want of taste which could produce so pert, so worldly a heroine as the beloved of such a man as Darcy.[18]

As a fellow author Mitford highly valued Jane Austen's skill as a novelist. In the same letter she remarks:

> I quite agree with you in preferring Miss Austen to Miss Edgeworth. If the former had a little more taste, a little more perception of the graceful, as well as of the humorous, I know not indeed any one to whom I should not prefer her. There is none of the hardness, the cold selfishness, of Miss Edgeworth about her writings; she is in a much better humour with the world; she preaches no sermons; she wants nothing but the *beau idéal* of the female character to be a perfect novel-writer. . . .[19]

With all her appreciation of the novelist, Mitford was too much imbued with the new prudish principles of the age to stomach Elizabeth's old rationality. We shall return to the significance of her reservations later, but here we may assume that her response to the heroine represented the dominant opinion of this period.

But if she was thus surrounded by enemies, Elizabeth had at least one strong supporter: the author. Born in 1775, Jane Austen grew up in the rational spirit of the eighteenth century, and Elizabeth is in a sense a spokesman of the novelist who must have felt intense discomfort in the new social climate after the turn of the century. The author's purpose in the book, however, is not merely to expose the irrationality of the new trend. One will readily admit that Elizabeth is by no means perfect; on the contrary, she has her own faults, making a series of mistakes, and this negative aspect of Elizabeth requires further consideration.

Of Elizabeth's faults, it is probably her overconfidence in herself that first draws the reader's attention. She certainly has neither the humility of Catherine Morland nor the introspective habit of Fanny Price, and her excessive trust in her own insight sometimes leads her to grievous errors, such as her misperception of Wickham's character. Her judgement there is indeed very hasty; she determines Wickham's goodness at the first meeting, without sufficient facts to go on. Yet we should not on our part hastily ascribe her misinterpretation to her overconfidence alone; as several critics point out, her partiality to Wickham is deeply connected with her dislike of Darcy.[20] In the scenes of his first appearance in the book Wickham behaves himself in an exactly opposite way to Darcy: Darcy is very formal and cold in manners, Wickham, easy and warm; Darcy varies his attitude towards others according to their rank, Wickham is invariably amicable to everybody. And since she has a pet aversion to Darcy who thus attaches too much weight to social values, she is very favourably impressed on the rebound by Wickham who appears to her to value the intrinsic worth of an individual without reference to position or status. The underlying cause of her misperception of Wickham's character, therefore, is her strong antipathy towards Darcy—or, more precisely, her antipathy towards the irrational tendency in society in general of which she believes he is a representative. She holds that those who unduly stick to social forms are 'devoid of every proper feeling' (368), and this belief is so strong that she jumps to a hasty conclusion that those who do not worry about forms must have every virtue.

But if Elizabeth were merely favourably impressed by Wickham, her error might be comparatively small. As it is, in the succeeding interactions with him she falls into more serious confusions of judgement. Wickham is indeed indifferent to forms, but his indifference is in fact not a judicious indifference, as Elizabeth expects, but a careless and thoughtless one. He is presumptuous in manners and insincere in professions; he readily reveals past private affairs in his benefactor's household to a stranger, and would not mind even disgracing the family in public. Originally loose in morals, he is indiscriminate in infringing the rules of propriety. Even if she could not know his real character, therefore, Elizabeth should at least have noticed this dangerous tendency that is openly presented before her; but her wish to believe in his goodness makes her blind to all this. Furthermore, she even attempts to vindicate his most glaring misconduct. He is at first markedly attentive to Elizabeth, but when he hears that a Miss King has acquired 10,000 pounds, he suddenly discards Elizabeth to woo this lady. Far from being offended at this evident mercenariness, however, Elizabeth tries to justify his conduct. To her aunt who mildly censures him for his 'indelicacy', Elizabeth retorts: 'A man in distressed circumstances has not time for all those elegant decorums which other people may observe' (153). Here she utterly confuses the flexible attitude towards the rules of behaviour with the disregard of them; her opinion has been that one should not unduly adhere to forms, but her too strong hatred of the inflexible adherents disorders her judgement and causes her to incline to anarchism. An antipathy towards undue adherence to forms has been turned unawares in her to an antipathy towards forms themselves.[21]

In a similar way, her abhorrence of undue adherence to rank makes Elizabeth blind to the *raison d'être* of rank in society. In the hierarchical society of the time the division of status was apt to be regarded as a classification of men, but this by no means annulled its essential function—the distribution of social roles: one's rank was indeed an emblem of one's role in society. Naturally, the higher one's rank, the greater one's social responsibility was, and those in a privileged position who did not need to earn a living—the landowners—were especially under the heavy obligation of public service. Concerning the landowners' general stance in society, G. E. Mingay remarks that, although they 'showed the obvious defects of a ruling aristocracy', such as 'pride' and 'some degree of contempt for the "lower orders"', they were 'generally conscientious in public office' and did not 'overlook their duties towards those in their hands, their tenants and servants, the poor, and the community as a whole'.[22] They had a good side as well as a bad one, then, and this is quite true with Darcy and Lady Catherine in the novel; they are haughty and sometimes unjustly dictatorial, but they are also conscientious and responsible landowners. Yet Elizabeth's eye is directed only to their bad side—their hauteur or 'contempt for the lower orders'—and is unmindful of the social significance of their rank. She is apparently indifferent to Lady Catherine's public activities which she witnesses during her stay at Hunsford (169), and until she visits Pemberley she associates Darcy's wealth and status with nothing but obnoxious pride. Her belief that one's rank has nothing to do with one's intrinsic worth is certainly reasonable, but her hatred of undue sticking to rank goes so far that, quite insensible to what a rank stands for in terms of social organization, she grows disgusted with the existence of rank itself.

Thus Elizabeth, with her deep repugnance against the over-adherence to social forms, loses her balance and inclines to an anarchic posture. But her over-reaction is checked before it goes too far: Darcy's letter awakens her to the impropriety which has often manifested itself in Wickham's conduct, and her visit to Pemberley helps her to become aware of the social responsibility that is attached to Darcy's rank. As a result of this realization, she now begins to shake off her undue hatred of forms themselves. In the course of her recovery, though, she has to experience bitter humiliation. 'Till this moment, I never knew myself', cries she after the perusal of Darcy's letter (208); she must now admit that she has totally lost sight of herself. Indeed, her mental isolation has driven her to a series of self-delusions. When she is forced to fight a solitary battle with the world, she apparently presents no gloomy image of a lonely fighter like Marianne Dashwood; she rather tries to assume the role of a detached satirist. In reality, however, she cannot achieve that detachment; behind her ridicule lies a bitter feeling that her own views, which she believes to be right, are not accepted, and in spite of her seemingly courageous attitude in setting at nought the opinion of the world, she has a deep-seated desire for approbation. And this mentality promotes her blindness. Her depreciation of Darcy and prizing of Wickham is a sort of demonstration to convince others of their wrongness and her rightness, but her impatient and exasperated mind causes confusion in her judgement; she condemns any adherence and applauds any indifference to forms indiscriminately, and when she comes to herself, she realizes that she has far diverged from her usual self. She deplores her thoughtless impetuosity, and with good reason; at the same time, there is much to sympathize with in her solitary struggle.

In connection with this solitary struggle of Elizabeth and its consequent effect on her mentality, it is worth referring here to a book by Muriel Jaeger called *Before Victoria*. As we have already seen, English social life underwent a radical change from the late eighteenth century to the early nineteenth century, and based on the ample evidence found in individual life stories Jaeger argues that the abrupt change of social character caused confusion of mind in many people; they were 'caught', says she, 'between the standards, morals and tastes of the Age of Reason and those of the Victorian Age',[23] and a person whom Jaeger mentions as representative of the 'caught' generation is Mary Russell Mitford. Born in 1787, 'Mary Mitford's environment as a girl was free and pleasant in the old style' (130); but later in the 1810s when she was obliged to support her family by writing, she could not 'escape the wave of Pauline prudishness in which she had to work and earn her living' (134). While appreciating the skill of Jane Austen, therefore, she could not bring herself wholly to accept the taste of the twelve-year-older novelist, whose 'propriety was still nearer to the common-sense propriety of the eighteenth century than to the new prudish propriety of the nineteenth' (127). In Mitford's ambivalent attitude towards her senior author Jaeger discerns a sign of 'muddle-headedness' peculiar to the 'caught' people (129).

But the effect of the rapid change in social climate was sometimes more devastating. In the chapter entitled 'A Schizoid Society' Jaeger demonstrates, taking the example of Caroline Lamb who was notorious for her scandalous love affair with Byron, how those caught people were driven to desperation as a result of emotional struggle, and notes that the Regency period (1811–20) witnessed remarkable prevalence of libertinism—the multiplication of scandals, the ubiquity of ruined gamblers, the increase of duels, the craze for prize-fighting, and so on—as if 'eighteenth-century freedom and tolerance had worked itself up into a frenzy of perversity and dissipation' (73). Contemporary observers seem to have been much perplexed at their society, in which licentiousness thus grew in the midst of the vast improvement of manners and morals, and Jaeger quotes Hannah More, who wrote in 1818: 'It appears to me that the two classes of character are more decided than they were; the wicked seem more wicked, and the good, better' (74). The people were polarized into the good and the bad in consequence of the new rigidity of social life.

It may be obvious now that Jane Austen delineated Elizabeth Bennet against this social background. Although Elizabeth recovers herself before going too far, the way in which she is gradually losing herself and inclining to an anarchic attitude owing to her emotional revolt against society is indeed suggestive of the fate of a number of the unsteady minds in this period that were caught between the old style and the new. For those who had deeply committed themselves to the eighteenth-century freedom and rationality, the rapidly formalizing social life after the turn of the century was hard—even impossible—to be reconciled to, and when they found themselves isolated in society, they resorted to desperate acts. Jane Austen was of course well aware of the importance of forms as maintainers of social order, but she also knew that too much formalization—especially when it happened suddenly—would incur revolt and eventually produce a consequence which was the exact opposite of the intention of those who furthered it: that is, loss of orderliness instead of its advancement. Hannah More might wonder why licentiousness prevailed in spite of the immense progress of reformation of manners and morals, but it was clear to the shrewd observer that it was precisely this sudden crystallization of manners and morals that caused the swelling of recklessness. It is interesting, therefore, that Elizabeth should finally achieve happiness by marrying Darcy, who has discarded his undue adherence to social forms; if Darcy represents society and Elizabeth the 'caught' people in this period, Darcy's conversion means the normalization of society, and Elizabeth's marriage with him suggests the reconciliation of the isolated minds to their society. This denouement indicates, that is, the course which the author wished her society to take, and their harmonious married life in Pemberley is a symbolic picture of a society in which order is restored. It seems, however, that Jane Austen felt this ending rather too optimistic; in her next work, *Mansfield Park*, she was again to deal with the same problem as was taken up in *Pride and Prejudice*, but this time she became far more serious and stern in expressing a warning to her society.

CHAPTER 4

The Other Side of an Orderly World: *Mansfield Park*

Every reader of *Mansfield Park* must remember the scene where the young people in the midst of their theatrical bustle are petrified by the unexpected return of Sir Thomas Bertram. The scene is certainly dramatic and the sudden termination of the boisterous frolic impresses us afresh with the extent of the master's dominance as a moral authority. Indeed, in his imposing dignity and rigorousness Sir Thomas is quite unique among Jane Austen's characters, and likewise unparalleled is the sober atmosphere of Mansfield Park which is under his absolute sway. In interpreting the novel this unusual setting is a very important factor and what significance it has is a matter requiring careful consideration. Interestingly enough, despite the notorious diversity of opinions on *Mansfield Park*, there seems to be an agreement among critics concerning this point. Many of them regard Sir Thomas as a man cast in the old mould and Mansfield Park as a world representative of the traditional values of eighteenth-century England; and usually this 'oldness' is contrasted with the 'newness' of the interlopers, the Crawfords. (Based on this assumption, critical discussion has mainly been focused on the problem of whether Jane Austen was a defender or a critic of tradition.) Yet there is room for reconsideration. One important fact about Sir Thomas and Mansfield Park is that there is not a single word or phrase in their description that associates them with the past. Sir Thomas does not show any tendency to stick to the old ways of life, nor is the house old—indeed, it is 'modern-built' (48). If they are meant to stand for old values, this is certainly odd. But of course the prevailing critical assumption relies not so much on this kind of direct reference as on a certain ethos, such as strict decorum and rigid morality; these elements, however, which are commonly considered symbolic of the former age, are in fact closely related with the new social climate of early nineteenth-century England.

Mansfield Park was written during 1811–13, and, as we have seen in the previous chapter, by the time Jane Austen began the novel English society had altered a great deal from what it had been in the last years of the eighteenth century. The most momentous change in this period was brought about by material growth. The Industrial Revolution which had started in the latter half of the century began to shake the country's economic system to its foundation, and the rise of those classes engaged in trade and industry was markedly accelerated. The late eighteenth and early nineteenth century was indeed an epoch of rapid social transition. While those economic and structural changes went on, however, another important revolution was taking place in English society—a remarkable 'improvement' in manners and morals, which has an important bearing on the world depicted in the novel. To get a clear view of the link between them let us here briefly retrace the steps this revolution took in this period.[1] The central force behind this remarkable phenomenon was the energetic activities of ardent reformers, the Evangelicals. Beginning as a small group within the Established Church, their numbers, scope of activities, and influence vastly increased from the 1790s onward; unlike the earlier and rather idealistic reformers of the eighteenth century, they were remarkably practical and their activities highly organized, employing various tactics and strategies to advance the 'reform' of the nation. But what was particularly favourable to their cause was the peculiar political atmosphere of the time which the impact of the French Revolution produced in England. The reactionary ruling classes considered that political stability must be maintained not only through the reinforcement of law and order but also through the regulation of manners, as they saw, or thought they saw, a strong link between immorality and liberalism in France. The Evangelicals took advantage of this political climate; indeed, their propaganda was so successful that 'Reform or Ruin' became even a popular rallying cry. Thus the religious and moral teachings of the reformers

CHAPTER 4

With its strict rules of behaviour dominating, Mansfield Park does not appear to be a very comfortable place to live in, and for the Bertram children—for the girls at least—its atmosphere is somewhat suffocating. This code of manners is of course imposed by Sir Thomas, the head of the family; it is worth noting, however, that the imposition is not exactly a coercion—the children are in a sense even willing to comply. For Maria and Julia good manners are an important part of their accomplishments and, therefore, an indispensable token of their social status. All the same, they have a strong feeling of being restrained; after all, they lack the inner morality that ought to sustain outward manners. It is this ambiguous, paradoxical mentality that marks the girls' feelings at their father's departure to Antigua: 'without aiming at one gratification that would probably have been forbidden by Sir Thomas, they felt themselves immediately at their own disposal, and to have every indulgence within their reach' (32). With Sir Thomas leaves an imposer of burdens, but, for their own sake, they for a while choose to keep up their decorous behaviour. And yet a deep desire to break the chain always lies hidden in their minds, and the first volume puts into focus the process in which this latent desire gradually comes to the surface.

During the trip to Sotherton Maria suffers bitterly, having been defeated in a silent battle with her sister for the box seat of the barouche; and though her irritation is barely subdued according to 'her own sense of propriety' (81), here we sense the presence of potential subversive energy. This situation in which lurking disruptive forces are struggling to burst through restrictions illustrates the disease corroding Mansfield, and through the succeeding occurrences at Sotherton the seriousness of the condition is represented metaphorically and with masterly skill.[2] At Sotherton the party from Mansfield is first shown round the house: a number of lofty rooms fitted with magnificent but out-of-date furniture and decked with numerous family portraits which are 'no longer any thing to any body' (85); the old chapel at which services are no longer held—all these are tokens of ostensible dignity and stiff formality void of substance, like correct manners and strict decorum without moral backing. Naturally, these scenes give the visitors a feeling of oppression: on finding a door leading to the garden, 'as by one impulse, one wish for air and liberty, all walked out' (90). But their escape does not stop there; from the lawn 'bounded on each side by a high wall' (90), the young people move on and go down to the wilderness, as if searching for more liberty. Then, in the wilderness, another significant incident takes place. At the bottom of it and over the ha-ha there is an iron gate—a symbol of circumscribing rules of behaviour enforced. Sitting at the bench in front of it, Maria complains: 'that iron gate, that ha-ha, give me a feeling of restraint and hardship. I cannot get out, as the starling said' (99).[3] Her express desire to pass through the gate to the park induces Mr Rushworth to go to fetch the key; but Maria, not waiting his return, passes round the edge of the gate with the help of Henry Crawford—an act indicative of infringement of the code of propriety. Soon after, Julia also scrambles across the fence to follow them. Thus, although no serious violation of decorum actually occurs at Sotherton, a series of significant incidents effectively suggests the impatience of restraint that is growing inside Mansfield Park.

These impulses are at last unleashed in the form of 'acting'. The theatrical scheme, once initiated, thoroughly engrosses all the young people, except Edmund and Fanny; but there is a certain difference in mentality between the Bertram children and the others. The Crawfords and Mr Yates are outsiders who are not subject to the law of Mansfield, and their ardour is simply an enthusiasm for acting. But the case of the Bertrams is more complicated: they are responsible members of the family, and they know that acting is against the Mansfield code of decorum—it is precisely a 'gratification that would probably have been forbidden by Sir Thomas'; and yet the very fact that it is so inflames their passion. For the sisters especially, the theatricals furnish an excellent opportunity to fulfil their long repressed desire for liberty. Indeed, the idea of acting stirs the dormant forces inside Mansfield Park, and the unleashed energy, supported by the fervour of the outsiders, impels 'their darling project' (158) forward. It is a project pregnant with dangerous consequences, however; as might be expected of such impetuous actions, disorder manifests itself gradually as the scheme advances. Order is of course closely associated with rules of behaviour; the increasing indecorum during this episode is therefore worth particular notice. The attempt at acting itself is 'improper', and so is the play selected; but Maria, in justification of these, dexterously distorts the notion of decorum. To Edmund who urges her to set the example of 'true delicacy' by giving up the scheme, she retorts: 'I really cannot undertake to harangue all the rest upon a subject of this kind.—*There* would be the greatest indecorum I think' (140). On the other hand, during a series of loud discussions about the selection of the play and casting, civility in general is driven to the edge of dissolution. This atmosphere draws out each person's selfishness—though still 'more or less disguised' (131)—and induces Julia's angry detachment from the scheme. Evidently the weakening ties of the code of manners promote disharmony. Meanwhile, the stage preparations cause a physical disturbance in the house. Then the rehearsals start, and the confusion reaches its culmination. The players are placed 'on a footing which must do away all restraints' (154), and the disappearance of fetters has the final liberating effect upon their minds. While 'rehearsing all over the house' (169), they entirely give way to their feelings:

> Fanny, being always a very courteous listener, and often the only listener at hand, came in for the complaints and distresses of most of them. . . . So far from being all satisfied and all enjoying, she found every body requiring something they had not, and giving occasion of discontent to the others. (164–65)

The collapse of external supports brings about ugly clashes between unrestrained egos. The orderly world of Mansfield Park is transformed into sheer moral anarchy.

By illustrating the inevitability of wild disorder when rules of behaviour are nullified, the theatrical episode teaches us a simple truth about human society: rules are indispensable. But it also reveals the vehemence of the impulse to defy the truth. As we have seen, Jane Austen carefully charts this impulse from its early signs to the final eruption, with the implication that the presence of such menacing energy puts Mansfield Park in a very precarious position. To understand the meaning of all this, we must now look into the causes of the growth of this strong impulse. And it is the character of Sir Thomas, the lawgiver of Mansfield Park, that furnishes a key.

Sir Thomas's exactness is stressed frequently: he has a 'measured manner' (240), 'correctly punctual habits' (222), and '[h]is sense of decorum is strict' (127). Moreover, his 'dignified manner . . . keeps every body in their place' (162). Obviously the control of his children with such rigidity is one of the reasons for their rebellion; but it does not account for everything—the problem is deeper. It was suggested earlier that the sisters' impatience of restraint is to a large degree due to lack of morality, and this lack is perhaps inevitable, because their father himself shares the defect. In the opening paragraph of the book which gives an account of the fates of the Ward sisters there is a significant passage:

> Sir Thomas Bertram had interest, which, from *principle* as well as *pride*, from *a general wish of doing right*, and *a desire of seeing all that were connected with him in situations of respectability*, he would have been glad to exert for the advantage of Lady Bertram's sister. . . . (3–4; emphasis added)

The juxtaposition of the two kinds of motives—one moral and philanthropic, the other worldly and ambitious—is indeed prophetic. Sir Thomas believes in being ethical—even prides himself that he is a man of strict morality; and yet his moral sense tends to be suppressed or smothered by his worldly ambition, so that he fails to live up to his own ideals, often on occasions of critical importance. His connivance at Maria's loveless marriage with the dull-witted Mr Rushworth is one example. On finding the man a very poor match for his daughter, Sir Thomas feels that, '[a]dvantageous as would be the alliance . . . her happiness must not be sacrificed to it' (200). When Maria, however, who 'was less and less able to endure the restraint which her father imposed' (202), assures him of her 'highest esteem for Mr. Rushworth's character and disposition',

> Sir Thomas was satisfied; *too glad to be satisfied perhaps to urge the matter quite so far as his judgment might have dictated to others*. It was an alliance which he could not have relinquished without pain. . . . (200–01; emphasis added)

Thus Sir Thomas readily yields to the irresistible appeal of an advantageous alliance; his moral judgement ceases functioning at Maria's specious pretense. And to reconcile himself to all this, he has recourse to a strained interpretation of her disposition, which, of course, is far from the truth. Justly enough, this easy concession—the wilful distortion of his own judgement—is to be bitterly rewarded with Maria's scandalous elopement.

But a more impressive instance of the digression from integrity is seen in his labour to promote another marriage of convenience—the marriage between Fanny and Henry Crawford. This time he more actively engages himself in the business and the suspension of his moral judgement becomes the more serious in nature, though by no means conspicuous or easily discernible. The way he first notices Henry's particular attentions to Fanny is represented in this manner:

> and though infinitely above scheming or contriving for any the most advantageous matrimonial establishment that could be among the apparent possibilities of any one most dear to him, and disdaining even as a littleness the being quick-sighted on such points, he could not avoid perceiving in a grand and careless way that Mr. Crawford was somewhat distinguishing his niece—nor perhaps refrain (though unconsciously) from giving a more willing assent to invitations on that account. (238)

About this passage R. A. Cox remarks that 'here she [Jane Austen] is doing more than use Sir Thomas's language to describe Sir Thomas: she has slipped into a quotation of his thoughts, or perhaps less his conscious thoughts than his assumptions about himself'.[4] Indeed, in this subtle narration the author cunningly conveys how Sir Thomas, despite his ostensible contempt of worldly calculation, is captivated with the prospect of the 'advantageous' match, and from this moment his words and deeds are continuously accompanied with gross self-deception and far-fetched self-justification. At first he would not admit to himself that he is 'contriving' the match; he decides to hold a ball at Mansfield—to give Henry an opportunity to court Fanny, really, but he deludes himself into believing that it is to gratify 'William's desire of seeing Fanny dance' (252). Then, obliged to be conscious of his purpose, he pleads Fanny's interest, obliterating the trace of calculation from his mind; while communicating Henry's proposal to Fanny he assumes that 'he must be gratifying her far more than himself' (314). Finally, meeting with Fanny's refusal to accept Henry (which is a tacit reproof of the selfishness of his scheme), he lays the blame on the innocent niece. The scene in the East room where he egotistically reprimands Fanny is indeed the climax of the novel, and he himself exposes his unjustness when, soon afterwards, he labels Mrs Norris's remarks on Fanny as unjust, although they exactly coincide with his attack on Fanny. Thus Sir Thomas, by means of self-deception, commits glaring transgressions against his own moral principles without the slightest awareness of the fact, and this unconscious hypocrisy, as Jane Nardin terms it,[5] is a predominant feature of his character. It is hardly to be wondered at, therefore, that his daughters should be deficient in moral sense.

Outwardly very strict, but lax enough within—these two aspects of Sir Thomas, though apparently paradoxical, are of course closely linked together: his wish to persuade himself as well as others that he is a man of principle necessitates the polishing of manners, which are supposed to be an outward manifestation of inward morality. External strictness is a compensation, as it were, for internal laxity, and actually his belief—or illusion—that a perfect exterior indicates a perfect interior supports his very existence. Similarly, the world of Mansfield Park itself depends on this illusion for its maintenance. It is a world of order, certainly; but beneath its 'external smoothness' is concealed 'the want of real harmony' (191). In the final analysis, Sir Thomas's hold over his family is confined to the sphere of outward behaviour. As is the case with himself, he is satisfied with his daughters' outer perfection—'in person, manner, and accomplishments' (20)—and is unaware of their deficiencies within. But a facade without inner support is subject to collapse; as David Lodge argues, propriety which is not animated by moral principles is fragile.[6] For the daughters the strict code of behaviour imposed on them is no less than a shackle, and their respect for it merely as a status symbol is too weak a motive for them to bear its restriction all the time. Their rebellion is a natural result of an unnatural form of control.

But if Sir Thomas is a man of strict morals only in appearance, one wonders why he should try to put on such a semblance in the first place. Obviously the problem has a deep connection with the social circumstances of the age, and in fact much of the author's intention of social criticism is concerned there. The growth of the national ardour for moral reform seemed to bring about a remarkable improvement in English social life around the turn of the century; yet one is inclined to doubt if such radical refashioning of moral character of a nation is really possible, and I think Jane Austen's acute sensitivity not only led her to a full awareness of the phenomenon, but also enabled her to realize its superficiality. We could reason this way: perceiving that what people believed to be an improvement in morals was really a mere adjustment of outward behaviour, the novelist tried to embody the national illusion in the figure of Sir Thomas. The baronet's perverse adherence to the semblance of strict morals becomes intelligible if it is seen as a piquant picture of a 'reformed' society.

Yet this unmasking of hypocrisy is not the whole of Jane Austen's criticism of her society; by describing in detail how fragile is the order that depends only on regulation of behaviour, the novelist also suggests the possibility of its self-destruction. That a code of manners is inoperative where supportive moral values are deficient, that a rigorous enforcement of it often invites impetuous disobedience—this admonition was no doubt directed at the contemporary society. In fact, the disorder of society implied in the theatrical episode had a real counterpart. In parallel with the growth of new rigid standards, the 1810s witnessed a notable increase in licentiousness as well; the Regency was indeed full of scandals, duels, gambling, and frantic pleasure-hunting, as though 'eighteenth-century freedom and tolerance had worked itself up into a frenzy of perversity and dissipation', as Muriel Jaeger puts it.[7] Evidently the excessive purification of social life was calling forth desperate reaction in the early nineteenth century. Jane Austen's concern for social order expressed in the novel was by no means exaggerated.

Let us now turn our attention to Fanny Price, the heroine of the book, and consider her character from the viewpoint of the author's intent, social criticism. Fanny is of course an important person in the novel, and yet her importance is a little different in nature from such active heroines as Elizabeth Bennet or Emma Woodhouse. Just as she herself is quiet and unobtrusive, so is her role in the book characterized by passivity. She is, as it were, a moral gauge for the other characters, and their defects—for they are more or less defective—are often highlighted by the contrast with her unexceptionable character. The Crawfords' amorality, for instance, appears all the more glaring when it is placed side by side with Fanny's strict morality. But a subtler and more important contrast is seen between Fanny and the inhabitants of Mansfield Park. Unlike the Crawfords who openly flaunt their amorality, the Bertrams at least assume an air of conformity to the moral code; nonetheless, they all deviate from the narrow path, with the exception of the utterly inactive Lady Bertram. Fanny, on the other hand, seldom goes astray; in fact, she is the only person in Mansfield Park who lives up to its moral ideals. As to the causes of the Bertrams' transgressions we have already observed: Tom, Maria, and Julia lack principles themselves, and Sir Thomas tends to suppress his moral sense. Even Edmund shows a tendency to unconscious hypocrisy; from time to time he too sacrifices his principles for self-interest, as is seen in his participation in the theatrical scheme and his attempt to coax Fanny into accepting Henry's proposal. On these occasions his judgement is warped by his infatuation with Mary Crawford. But Fanny is free from those weaknesses; she not only possesses solid moral principles but also makes strenuous efforts to act in accordance with their dictates. During the theatrical episode, for example, she examines her own actions and motives very strictly, asking herself whether she is right to refuse the others' joint request for her playing a part in the play, and whether her refusal is based purely on her moral judgement:

> She had begun to feel undecided as to what she *ought to do*.... Was she *right* in refusing what was so warmly asked, so strongly wished for? what might be so essential to a scheme on which some of those to whom she owed the greatest complaisance, had set their hearts? Was it not ill-nature—selfishness—and a fear of exposing herself? And would Edmund's judgment, would his persuasion of Sir Thomas's disapprobation of the whole, be enough to justify her in a determined denial in spite of all the rest? It would be so horrible to her to act, that she was inclined to suspect the truth and purity of her own scruples.... (152–53)

Indeed, Fanny's habit of strict self-scrutiny presents a striking contrast to her guardians' liability to self-deception, and from this results the marked difference in their conduct. What then is the meaning of the contrast between Fanny and the Bertrams? Since the difference lies in whether they can live up to their moral ideals or not, we could regard it as a contrast between the theory and practice of moral reform. That is, if Sir Thomas and his family represent the actual state of an ostensibly reformed society, Fanny is the ideal aimed at by the reformers and the rising public opinion in general; the juxtaposition makes palpable the gap between the ideal and reality of the reform movement of the period.

Jane Austen had her doubts, it seems, as to the soundness of the reform movement itself. It is worth noting that Sir Thomas surrenders his principles chiefly for the welfare of the 'family'. Considering that one of the incentives for moral reform in this age was the urgent necessity to maintain the existing social order, Sir Thomas's acts are very significant, since they demonstrate the incompatibility of social and moral interests. This reveals, then, an essentially self-contradictory aspect of the reform movement of the day. Furthermore, in the contrast between Fanny and the Bertrams is implied the author's disbelief in moral improvement. Fanny is by no means a lifeless incarnation of virtue; she has her own little weaknesses, and the novelist obviously takes pains to depict her as a human being. One could say that Fanny is a character in whom the moral ideals of the age are realized as far as humanly possible. From this, however, it does not necessarily follow that she was meant for an exemplary figure; rather, her efforts at self-denial, which sometimes look almost superhuman, serve to suggest how inordinate the moral demands of the period were. Indeed, to the modern reader the moral books of this age—Hannah More's works, for instance, with which Jane Austen was familiar—appear absurdly over-scrupulous and narrow-minded, and some contemporary readers seem to have reacted to them similarly. In her diary Fanny Burney comments on Hannah More's *Thoughts on the Importance of the Manners of the Great to General Society* (1788) thus: 'The design is very laudable, and speaks a mind earnest to promote religion and its duties; but it sometimes points out imperfections almost unavoidable, with amendments almost impracticable'.[8] This comment on a book whose author was to become a leading Evangelical aptly summarizes the nature of the whole reform movement of the day: it was an impracticable attempt. In her letter to Cassandra written in 1809 Jane Austen professes her dislike of the Evangelicals;[9] she was no doubt impatient of their brazen-faced assurance in imposing their self-righteous doctrines on the population (and this sentiment, as we have seen in Chapter 1, was later manifested in the innuendo that is cast at these reformers in the novel-defending passage in *Northanger Abbey*). The contrast between Fanny and the Bertrams, therefore, not only indicates the flaws in society, but suggests the excessiveness of the moral ideals imposed on it. Apparently Fanny has affinities with the virtuous heroines of the didactic novels of the time, such as Lucilla Stanley in Hannah More's *Cœlebs in Search of a Wife* (1808) or Laura Montreville in Mary Brunton's *Self Control* (1811); under the cover of the prevailing didacticism, however, a poignant social criticism was wide awake. Fanny's moral perfection, which is represented as a product of extraordinary self-restraint, carries the implication that it would be preposterous to expect such perfection from the whole of society; Sir Thomas's hypocrisy intimates, therefore, that this is the inevitable result of the credulous acceptance of the impracticable teachings of the reformers.

Thus Jane Austen, with her shrewd practical eye, insinuates her mistrust of the specious attempt at moral reform; satirizes the society which, encouraging the attempt, has fallen into an illusion of improvement; and warns of the possible disintegration of such a self-complacent society. With this understanding, we can now have a clearer view of the Crawfords. In our attempt to place the dramatis personae in historical context, we have linked the characters of the Crawfords to the old society. If the moral stiffness of Mansfield Park is a reflection of the new trend, their outspoken amorality is certainly reminiscent of the careless freedom of the eighteenth century. Of course, they were by no means an extinct species; on the contrary, their kind did flourish in Regency London, where the notorious Beau Brummell and other 'dandies' reigned over the fashionable society. Yet the licentious frenzy of this period was, so to speak, a last spark of dying embers; in the midst of the growing national ardour for improvement in manners and morals, the carefree attitude, rapidly being repressed, desperately burst out, noticeably in the metropolis. In a sense, therefore, London in the 1810s was rather behind the times; at least, it was a place least influenced by the reform movement of the period. Amateur theatricals, for instance, which had been in vogue in the 1780s throughout the country, petered out after the turn of the century owing to severe attacks from moralists, but in London they were still being performed in the 1810s.[10] 'It is not there [in London]', as Edmund significantly remarks, 'that respectable people of any denomination can do most good' (93). And so the Crawfords, coming down from London, bring with them the vices of the past that still survived and even thrived in that great city. To them, however, the inhabitants of Mansfield are on the whole favourably disposed. It is Fanny alone who perceives and is constantly on her guard against the danger they pose; the others allow themselves to be enchanted with their superficial attractions, and, in so doing, expose their weaknesses. The Bertram sisters' lack of principles manifests itself when they flirt with Henry Crawford. Edmund too, enamoured with Mary, reveals his frailty. Indeed, when her influence distorts his moral judgement and leads him into self-interested acts, Edmund's morals are almost on a level with those of Mary. But, of course, it is Sir Thomas who is induced to betray himself most ignominiously. As we have examined, dazzled by Henry's fortune and social status, Sir Thomas plots a marriage between Fanny and Henry, intent only on material advantages of the union, though his real purpose is disguised in his mind. Here again we are shown that Mansfield morality is in fact no better than that of the 'depraved' Londoners. Obviously, then, the author introduces the interlopers from London, not to denounce the corruption of metropolitan life, but to let them reveal the moral bankruptcy of Mansfield Park; they shake a facade off from Mansfield.

But if the Crawfords ruffle Mansfield, it, in turn, ruffles them. The moral seriousness of Mansfield, however superficial it may be, is still something new to the Londoners, and, in fact, it greatly affects their thought and behaviour. In Mary Crawford especially we can observe curious fluctuations. From the moment of her appearance in the book Mary demonstratively identifies herself with the London style; it is the only way of life that she has ever known, and in her new surroundings she tries to stick to it. And yet, strangely enough, she becomes attached to Edmund. At first she decides to attach herself to Tom because of his sophisticated manners and his status as an eldest son: 'She knew it was her way' (47). In spite of herself, however, her heart soon inclines to the inconspicuous younger son, who is 'not pleasant by any common rule' (65). 'There was a charm, perhaps,' the narrator comments, 'in his sincerity, his steadiness, his integrity, which Miss Crawford might be equal to feel, though not equal to discuss with herself' (65). Sincerity, steadiness, integrity—these are things Mary has had no notion of, but she is unaccountably attracted by their indefinable charm; this is the beginning of her trouble. The fact that she prefers Edmund to Tom is no less than a deviation from the London code, yet there is worse to come: Edmund turns out to be a candidate for the clergy. It is definitely against her principle to marry a clergyman—'A clergyman is nothing' for her (92)—but, at the same time, she does not like to give up Edmund. Thus she is caught in a dilemma. To cut the Gordian knot she tries to discourage him from taking orders, recommending instead more fashionable professions, such as a lawyer, soldier, or sailor. Edmund, however, though otherwise ready to be influenced by her, is resolute on this particular point. Chagrined though she is, Mary is even disposed to concede, fancying that the country life might suit her; but in the picture she draws she must 'shut out the church, sink the clergyman, and see only the respectable, elegant, modernized, and occasional residence of a man of independent fortune' (248). Thus the country life she envisages is in fact a miniature London life, which can in no way accord with his future career. Here it is important to note that all along Mary fails to see the paradox in her struggle. In Edmund what originally attracts her is his moral integrity—a quality which is not to be found in London—and yet she tries to impose on him the London style and, therefore, annihilate the very source of his charm. Mary's problem is that, absorbed in the cultivation of style, she chooses not to realize what her heart really wants. Her struggle is futile.

Similarly, her brother Henry is also affected by Mansfield morals. Just as Mary is attracted by Edmund's probity, so is Henry charmed by Fanny's uprightness. Unlike his sister, he evinces no conscious adherence to London; but still he is a Londoner, who is unable to define the quality which fascinates him: 'Henry Crawford had too much sense not to feel the worth of good principles in a wife, though he was too little accustomed to serious reflection to know them by their proper name' (294). Obviously 'good principles' are beyond his ken, but perhaps their novelty, together with Fanny's resistance, is enough to excite his passion; no longer a cool 'flirt' (363), he now fervently courts Fanny. His headlong action indeed provides a contrast to his sister's lingering indecisiveness; since he does not know exactly what it is that he pursues, however, his impetuous courtship of Fanny is in a way as blind and ludicrous as Mary's hesitation to commit herself to Edmund. Henry is more active, and so his folly is more conspicuously exposed; but it seems that eventually they are equally worn out from their experiences at Mansfield Park; they struggle blindly only to exhaust themselves. With all their self-assurance, the Crawfords lose their way in an unknown land; and so must have done many people in the early nineteenth century who suddenly found themselves in a wholly transformed society.

❦

Let us finally consider Fanny's 'revolution of mind' (393) during her visit to Portsmouth. The turn of the story in this episode, curious and a little unexpected, presents one of the perplexing problems of the book, for one wonders why the author suddenly tries to vindicate the Mansfield way of life which she has hitherto rather condemned. Yet, just as the novelist does not really denounce the amateur theatricals—for, as our examination makes clear, it is not the right or wrong of the theatricals themselves that matters in the book—so does she not really extol Mansfield or disparage Portsmouth; the author's real aim in this episode is to suggest another harmful effect of the reform movement of this period, and to comprehend this, we should look closely at Fanny's feelings and behaviour at her parents' house.

The Price family sourly disappoints Fanny; they are vulgar, insensitive, selfish, and far from affectionate towards her. Moreover, the house itself—small, dirty, full of noise and confusion—causes her intolerable pains, both physical and mental. In short, almost everything in Portsmouth belies her expectation. At the same time, we should not overlook the curiously inflexible mentality of the heroine that underlies her disappointment. Fanny is, as Edmund remarks, 'of all human creatures the one, over whom habit [has] most power, and novelty least' (354); and actually, bound by the habits which she has acquired at Mansfield, she is unable to accommodate herself to the new surroundings. Indeed, Fanny is markedly inconsonant with the atmosphere of Portsmouth. During the first evening at her father's house her customary delicacy proves to be quite useless, but she pitifully keeps on practising it. Her moral judgement too, though it appears so proper at Mansfield, is rather out of place at Portsmouth. In her accustomed way she evaluates the character of each member of her family; but however sound her estimation may be, the exercise itself gives us an impression of incongruity. At Portsmouth what Fanny has hitherto considered to be essential to good life becomes meaningless, and her adherence to it appears even ridiculous, though deserving of sympathy. Perhaps in their nature the Prices and the Bertrams are not fundamentally different; there are even some similarities between them, notably between Lady Bertram and Mrs Price, as Fanny herself observes. Nevertheless, owing to the difference in manners, Portsmouth is quite different from Mansfield. At first Fanny tries to persuade herself that what matters is not forms but heart: 'manner Fanny did not want. Would they but love her, she should be satisfied' (377). Yet before long the squalid world of Portsmouth makes her realize that manners regulate not only behaviour but also heart; the crude lifestyle of Portsmouth brings out the worst in its inhabitants, as the sunshine in Portsmouth serves 'but to bring forward stains and dirt that might otherwise have slept' (439). And Fanny's mental habit is evidently too delicate to bear such exposed abjectness: 'After being nursed up at Mansfield, it was too late in the day to be hardened at Portsmouth' (413). It may be true that her disgust with her family leads her to exaggerate the merits of Mansfield; but what is important here is that behind her choice of Mansfield as 'home' lies the fact that her mind is so firmly formed in the Mansfield style that it cannot adapt itself to that of Portsmouth. And there lies the point of the whole episode: it does not comment on the right or wrong of the two worlds; it suggests the gulf between them.

At the beginning of the book the narrator remarks on the distinctness of the 'circles' in which the Bertrams and the Prices move (4), and Fanny's experience at Portsmouth does illustrate the width of the gulf that lies between the circles. In English society such dissociation between the classes began to manifest itself during the second half of the eighteenth century.[11] During the first half of the century, the gentry were by no means detached from the culture of the common people; in many ways the landed classes were still rustic and they frequently mingled with their inferiors on various occasions. After the middle of the century, however, intercourse between them became less frequent. Owing to the growing concern for 'refinement' among the upper classes, most gentlemen came to regard the rustic customs of the common people as coarse, vulgar, and uncivilized. Thus the two cultures gradually drew apart during the second half of the century. But the dissociation grew more conspicuous after the turn of the century. We have examined in the previous chapter how this trend is reflected in Darcy's proud contempt of his inferiors, and another good illustration of the rupture can be seen in the two contrasting depictions of Bath society in Jane Austen's works—one in *Northanger Abbey* and the other in *Persuasion*. As B. C. Southam points out, the Bath of the 1790s portrayed in *Northanger Abbey* is 'a social mixing-pot', in which people of different ranks—from families of wealthy landowners to those of lawyers or obscure clergymen—assemble together in the Public Rooms; whereas in the Bath of the 1810s depicted in *Persuasion* the gentry confine their social intercourse to the narrow range of their own circles.[12] This change in pattern of social intercourse was not restricted to Bath, but was a nation-wide phenomenon, and it was not a casual coincidence that its development ran parallel with the heightening of the national ardour for moral reform. As we have observed, the reform movement of this period, imperfect as it was, bore at least one notable result, namely, a remarkable improvement in manners. Yet the refinement of manners was no doubt a phenomenon concerned only with the affluent part of society. True, the reformers of this period devoted much of their energy to the improvement in tastes and morals of the common people, but, naturally, their exertion in that field had its limitations. Rather, the distinction of lifestyle between the rich and the poor became more and more apparent on account of the marked improvement in manners of the former; hence developed a solid barrier between their cultures. Indeed, the groundwork of what Disraeli later called 'the two nations' was already established during the early nineteenth century. Fanny's experience at Portsmouth—her bewilderment, disappointment, and incongruity with her own family—implies the seriousness of the social dissociation that came into being as a by-product of the reform movement.

At the end of the novel the unregenerate characters are banished from Mansfield Park and Fanny, rid of every obstacle, is happily united with Edmund. As a denouement this ending might be satisfactory, yet many of the problems that have been posed in the book seem to remain unsolved. Sir Thomas repents his worldly-mindedness, certainly; but still he is a moralistic (and very much evangelical) despot who would not forgive his daughter's offence—an offence which he admits to be the result of 'errors in his own conduct as a parent' (461). As long as such narrow-mindedness dominates, surely Mansfield will never escape the danger of relapsing into a place of empty morals. Similarly left unsettled is the problem of social severance. Fanny's sister Susan is received into Mansfield, but this can hardly be regarded as a token of the spiritual reunion of the two places; far from it, Susan is brought to Mansfield to be purged from the bad habits of Portsmouth—the gulf is as wide as ever. And then there are the Crawfords; apparently they are unable to accommodate themselves to the new moral climate after all. Thus the conclusion of the novel is on the whole rather evasive. And yet perhaps Jane Austen was satisfied with her diagnosis of the diseases of her society and dared not suggest remedies; in writing the last chapter she perhaps felt that all that should be said had already been said, and that there remained nothing but to conclude the story. At least the final chapter does round off the moral tale which she ingeniously uses as a cloak for social criticism. But certainly any little dissatisfaction does not prevent us from appreciating the keen insight and great skill of the novelist. The general trend of public opinion towards social purification was so powerful that what is called Victorianism was soon to be firmly established in England, and it is Jane Austen who first offered a penetrating criticism of that social phenomenon.

CHAPTER 5

Self-Deception and Superiority Complex:
Emma

In Jane Austen's novels we frequently encounter characters who disguise their real motives and intentions. In many cases the disguise is an unconscious one; unconsciously they replace unpalatable motives with palatable ones, and thus justify to themselves their own unpalatable acts. General Tilney is an absolute despot, but he usually exercises control over others covertly. In the scene of the conducted tour, he first takes Catherine outdoors, saying he 'yields' to her wishes as if it were 'against his own inclination' (*NA* 177); in fact, it is the General himself who wishes to go out, for it is his usual hour for a walk. It is indeed customary for the General to impose his will upon others under the cover of some specious pretexts. This sort of dissimulation is also discernible in Darcy in his act of separating Bingley from Jane. In his letter to Elizabeth he asserts that he did it solely for Bingley's sake. The reasons he adduces for disapproving of the union are convincing; but it is certainly not Bingley's advantage alone that actuates Darcy to force him to give up Jane. Priding himself on his abilities, he loves to dictate to others; this motivation is hidden, however, from himself as well as from others under the plausible pretext of saving Bingley. A further and yet more impressive instance of rationalization is found in Sir Thomas Bertram. As we have seen in the previous chapter, Sir Thomas is a man in whom a strong moral sense and worldly ambitions coexist, and on occasions—especially on occasions of importance—his moral sense is temporarily suspended. After the departure of Maria and Julia, Henry Crawford's courtship of Fanny becomes the main focus of the story, and the part Sir Thomas plays in this episode is very important, though by no means conspicuous. After noticing Crawford's particular attentions to his niece, Sir Thomas, 'though infinitely above scheming or contriving' (*MP* 238), encourages the intercourse with the Parsonage, holds the ball at his house, and, in providing favourable opportunities for the young man, paves the way for his proposal. His object in these exercises is of course to realize the 'advantageous' union (*MP* 238); Fanny is an instrument for extending his family's 'respectable alliances' (*MP* 20). But all the while he continues to disguise this motivation from himself. At first he will not even admit to himself that he is 'scheming or contriving'; he persuades himself that the ball is held to gratify 'William's desire of seeing Fanny dance' (*MP* 252). Then, obliged to acknowledge his intent, he deludes himself into believing that it is for Fanny's sake. When he communicates Crawford's proposal to Fanny, he imagines that 'he must be gratifying her far more than himself' (*MP* 314); and when confronted with her refusal, he flings quite unreasonable accusations at her.

General Tilney, Darcy, and Sir Thomas—the repeated portrayal of subtle self-justification in these characters indicates Jane Austen's deep interest in this behaviour pattern, and to the list of those self-deceiving characters, we can add yet another name, Emma Woodhouse. *Emma* was written immediately after *Mansfield Park*, and this time the heroine herself exhibits that tendency to dissemble her real motives, the most notable instance of which is found in her attempt at match-making. In her officious efforts to make a match between Harriet and Elton, Emma persuades herself into believing that she is acting for Harriet's sake. On their first meeting Emma decides to 'notice' this girl, and hatches the scheme then, as she later admits, of match-making for her as 'a very kind undertaking' (24). Then, to carry out this 'friendly arrangement of her own' (31), she tactfully leads Harriet into refusing Robert Martin's proposal. Indeed, her belief in her own 'kindness' does not falter in the slightest degree throughout the whole affair—not even when Mr Knightley severely criticizes her conduct; she argues to herself 'that let Mr. Knightley think or say what he would, she had done nothing which woman's friendship and woman's feelings would not justify' (67). 'Woman's friendship', however, is in fact quite irrelevant to the matter; Emma's match-making project is motivated by circumstances and inclinations that have nothing to do with Harriet—the absence of intellectual stimulus after Miss Taylor's marriage, a desire to display her own cleverness, a love of managing and arranging, and so on. Yet she would not admit those motivations to herself; instead, pleading Harriet's advantage, she perversely insists upon her 'good intentions' (99).

Emma's sophistry, like that of her predecessors, is a means of justifying her own conduct to herself; like them, she glosses over her unwarranted control of others by subtle manipulation of motives. This covert operation paralyses conscience, as it were; it enables one to commit acts which one could hardly commit with an easy conscience if one were fully cognizant of one's true motives—the substitute specious pretexts give sanction to any cruelty or injustice. This kind of rationalization is at the heart of most cases of tyranny, as we have seen in our examination of *Northanger Abbey*, where Jane Austen explores the problem of tyranny in terms of such self-justification. But in *Emma* her concern is not confined to the matter of unjust control of others alone. 'The neighborhood that did not exist in *Mansfield Park* is everywhere in *Emma*', as Claudia Johnson aptly observes, and this presence of 'neighbourhood' has an important meaning.[1] The novel gives a vivid and realistic picture of life in a rural community, and Emma, who attempts to tamper with the destinies of its inhabitants, is a disturber of the order of that community. Moreover, her meddling and mismanagement, though most noticeable in her match-making manoeuvre, are by no means restricted to that; in fact, with all her sensitivity to 'rank' or 'position', Emma's behaviour threatens to disrupt the system of hierarchy established in the community, and for a full appreciation of the matter we should carefully examine how far her mismanagement extends, and how her rationalizing is interrelated with it.

In the episode of the visit to Donwell Abbey there is a significant scene. In this excursion almost all the principal characters participate, and during the stroll in the pleasure grounds the ramblers, 'after walking some time over the gardens', assemble in 'the delicious shade of a broad short avenue of limes'. The narrator describes this avenue thus:

> It led to nothing; nothing but a view at the end over a low stone wall with high pillars, which seemed intended, in their erection, to give the appearance of an approach to the house, which never had been there. Disputable, however, as might be the taste of such a termination, it was in itself a charming walk, and the view which closed it extremely pretty. (360)

The avenue 'in itself' is 'a charming walk', but a curious part of it is its end, where there is 'a low stone wall with high pillars'; for they 'seemed intended, in their erection, to give the appearance of an approach to the house, which never had been there'. As Alistair Duckworth suggests, this walk at Donwell reminds one of the walk at Sotherton in *Mansfield Park*, and, like the wilderness with 'serpentine' paths and a 'locked' iron gate described there, this avenue with pillars of 'disputable taste' obviously bears some subtle implications.[2] A few pages before we are told that the house of Donwell Abbey 'looked what it was' (358); but here high pillars stand to give a false appearance—an appearance of an approach to the house which is not there. In connection with this matter of false appearances, Mr Knightley's behaviour in the scene deserves some notice: he walks tête-à-tête with Harriet. His object is to obtain better knowledge of her for Robert Martin's sake, but Harriet takes it as advances to herself. His manners, though unintentionally, give a false appearance—an appearance of an 'approach' to the girl who is not his aim. Yet it is not Mr Knightley's behaviour alone that presents a misguiding appearance; indeed, the book abounds with deceitful high pillars and non-existent houses.

In a scene before the lime-walk where the party take a rest in the shade, Jane Fairfax, harassed by Mrs Elton, who insists on her acceptance of a situation, is obliged to repeat 'the same motives' which she has urged before (359). These 'motives' are of course not genuine ones, if not utter lies; on account of her secret engagement with Frank Churchill, she is often compelled to evade and even deceive, and thus conjure up 'non-existent houses'. When her going to the post-office creates controversy, she pleads the salutary effects of the walk in order to conceal the real purpose of receiving Frank's letters unobserved. In a similar way her fiancé plays tricks on others. He goes to London, ostensibly to have his hair cut, but really to order a pianoforte for Jane. A more flagrant trick he plays is his use of Emma as a 'blind'; his ostentatious attentions to her are 'high pillars' to mislead others, and so Emma, a sham object, is a house which is not actually there. But, unlike Jane to whom such dissimulation is no less than a torment, Frank evidently derives fun from his histrionics; indeed, it is a dangerous but delightful game for him. Whether a torment or pleasure, however, they are both fully aware that they disguise their real motives; or rather, because of their awareness they suffer or enjoy. In Emma's case, on the other hand, there is no awareness in her dissimulation. She habitually erects 'high pillars', but she does it not so much to misdirect others as to misdirect herself. As we have noted, the most conspicuous instance of it is seen in her attempt at match-making between Harriet and Elton; but it is indeed only one instance—a part of a more complicated system of self-deception. 'Plain dealing was always best'—so Emma believes (341). But, if Frank Churchill's behaviour is marked by 'double dealing' (343), hers is characterized by what may be called unconscious double dealing. This double dealing of hers is closely connected with her excessive sensitiveness to 'rank' or 'position', and it is in fact more pernicious to the community of Highbury than Frank's 'conscious' double dealing.

There is a certain pattern in Emma's unconscious double dealing, and in order to discern this pattern—the way she erects 'high pillars'—it is important to understand the structural features of 'the old society'.[3] One's status in society signifies much in *Emma*, and of course it is Emma herself who is most particular about that. For other people, however, 'equality' or 'inequality' is a matter of no trivial importance; indeed, proper recognition of status is indispensable to daily intercourse among the inhabitants of Highbury. At the same time, it is in fact by no means simple or easy to recognize a person's status properly. In England in Jane Austen's day a small community such as a country village was the basic unit of society, and within each community 'a finely graded hierarchy of great subtlety and discrimination' was formed from a wealthy landowner down to the labouring poor. Such differentiation of status was generally accepted as a 'part of the given, unquestioned environment into which men were born'; but, owing to its 'great subtlety and discrimination', a precise order of precedence in the hierarchy was hardly determinable. People 'were acutely aware of their exact relation to those immediately above and below them'; with regard to the whole social structure, however, they had no more than vague concepts, such as the 'upper orders', the 'middling ranks', and 'labouring men'. Moreover, this complicated structure was rendered all the more complicated by remarkable social fluidity. The rise of rich merchants into the gentry was a familiar phenomenon in eighteenth-century England, while younger sons of the nobility and the gentry, who were obliged to enter professions and trades, constantly moved down into the middle ranks. Indeed, large-scale social mobility was a distinct characteristic of English society, where, at least until Waterloo (the year when *Emma* was completed), there were no palpable classes in the sense of mutually exclusive layers and so no strife between them; on the other hand, it certainly increased the complexity of the problem of status identification.

Highbury was meant, no doubt, to be an average country community of the day, and in the portrait of life in this village those features of the old society are quite accurately reflected. Highbury society is a graded status hierarchy, with a squire at the top and a destitute family living in a cottage at the bottom. The story chiefly concerns the upper levels (people in lower grades are only touched on now and then), but regardless of level the inhabitants seem content to live in the traditional framework of society— no rebellious feelings, no smouldering discontent detectable anywhere.[4] If the system of hierarchy itself is not questioned, however, the order of precedence within it is always a problem of great delicacy, which at times arouses controversy. Factors that determine social status are manifold, as indicated in Emma's resentful interior monologue after the scene of Mr Elton's proposal:

> he must know that in fortune and consequence she was greatly his superior. He must know that the Woodhouses had been settled for several generations at Hartfield, the younger branch of a very

> ancient family—and that the Eltons were nobody. The landed property of Hartfield certainly was inconsiderable, being but a sort of notch in the Donwell Abbey estate, to which all the rest of Highbury belonged; but their fortune, from other sources, was such as to make them scarcely secondary to Donwell Abbey itself, in every other kind of consequence; and the Woodhouses had long held a high place in the consideration of the neighbourhood which Mr. Elton had first entered not two years ago, to make his way as he could, without any alliances but in trade, or any thing to recommend him to notice but his situation and his civility. (136)

Here emerges a variety of elements on which the status of a family depends: descent and connections, the length of its residence, wealth and its source, occupation, and so on. To complicate matters further, some of those factors—such as income and official position—are subject to change. The intricacy which attends the process of status discrimination renders it practically impossible to determine an exact and permanent hierarchical order. Oliver MacDonagh sums up the case thus:

> Highbury classified itself internally in a precise though very complex fashion according to income, source of income, prescription, length of residence and function. On the other hand, this ideal arrangement is never matched exactly by the actual social order; or, more correctly, a fixed social order exists only as an abstract notion, or model, to be employed as a point of reference perhaps, but never realized.[5]

Indeed, the absence of a fixed social order is a circumstance which makes it convenient for Emma to rationalize her arbitrary behaviour.

Rank and position are a sort of obsession with Emma, and because of this preoccupation, as well as for the haughty and supercilious attitude she frequently shows, she has been often called a snob. Emma certainly has the appearance of a snob, and, in a sense, she may be one. But, strictly speaking, it is not snobbery that makes her obsessed with social discrimination. To ascertain the spring of her obsession it is necessary to observe carefully how she makes her judgments about the social position of the people around her. As the famous opening of the book points out, Emma enjoys many advantages, in natural attributes as well as in environment; she is endowed with acute mental powers, possesses a large fortune, and occupies a high place in the community she lives in. In addition, she has 'a disposition to think a little too well of herself' (5) and takes inordinate pride in her superiority. Also inordinate is her demand for others to acknowledge it; 'never loth to be first' (71), she is disposed not only to think a little too well of herself but also to expect others to think a little too well of her. In fact, it is her constant wish to stand 'always first and always right' in the eyes of those around her (84), and the avid desire for the recognition by others of her preeminence plays a key role in her personal relations; as Jane Nardin observes, 'virtually all of Emma's personal antipathies and preferences can be accounted for by the effects the person in question has upon Emma's self-esteem'.[6] Emma's choice of Harriet as a friend is determined by Harriet's 'very engaging' manner in 'shewing so proper and becoming a deference' to her (23). Jane Fairfax, on the other hand, inspires enmity in Emma, for her 'real' accomplishments and the high favour she wins among the inhabitants pose a threat to Emma's prominent position. Moreover, Jane is reserved and shows no flattering attitude towards Emma, which confirms the latter in her detestation.

It is important to note here that this highly subjective criterion is also applied to her judgment of social status; Emma's assessment of the position of others depends to a great degree on how they satisfy her sense of superiority. Harriet evinces blind adoration for Emma—'a flatterer in all her ways' (38)—and for this reason and with no other legitimate grounds she is pronounced 'a gentleman's daughter' (30). The notable difference in Emma's estimation of the social standing of the Westons and the Coles affords another illustration of this arbitrariness. Mr Weston and Mr Cole have both made their fortune in trade, and both have purchased estates in Highbury and settled there. Their careers are analogous, and so is their status in society; or, if there is any difference, it is that the Coles are wealthier, since they are now, 'in fortune and style of living, second only to the family at Hartfield' (207). The Coles have hitherto stayed at a respectful distance from Hartfield; but the reserve of this rising family, like that of the 'really accomplished' Jane Fairfax (166), appears to Emma's jealous eyes to be a token of rivalry. Consequently, they are held in contempt for their 'low origin' and regarded as 'only moderately genteel'; whereas the Westons, the avowed admirers of Emma, are counted among the 'regular and best families' in Highbury and so considered on an equal footing with the Knightleys and the Woodhouses (207). In the case of Elton, Emma's estimate drastically changes. At first Elton is also included, together with Mr Knightley and the Westons, among 'the chosen and the best' (20); indeed, during the period when he earns Emma's favour by his obsequious attentions, he is described as 'quite the gentleman himself . . . without low connections' (35). After showing 'presumption' by his courtship of Emma herself, however, he is relegated to being a 'nobody', with his relatives disparagingly mentioned as 'in trade' (136). Emma's severity towards the Coles somewhat softens after the dinner party at their house, where she is 'received with a cordial respect which could not but please, and given all the consequence she could wish for' (214); they are then acknowledged as 'worthy people' (231). But Mr Elton, once dismissed, never recovers his former high position.

One notes that 'trade', sometimes conveniently overlooked or disregarded, is at other times given great significance as a sign of 'low' standing; it serves as a handy tool which Emma uses to validate her arbitrary judgements. But 'trade' is not the only device available for her self-justification; Emma often converts her subjective judgements into objective facts, which she then employs as a means of justifying her own egocentric actions. As we have just seen, Harriet's status as a gentleman's daughter, determined according to Emma's peculiar criterion, is a pure invention. But once the determining process is obliterated from her mind, the invention gains objectivity as a 'fact', in which Emma obviously finds psychological support for her intimacy with a mere parlour-boarder of a common school. Furthermore, in her quarrel with Mr Knightley Emma makes use of this 'fact' to vindicate herself. Against Mr Knightley, who reproaches her for inducing Harriet to refuse Robert Martin's proposal, she pleads that

Robert Martin is not 'Harriet's equal' but 'undoubtedly her inferior as to rank in society'. The reason she adduces for Harriet's superiority is that 'her father is a gentleman' (61–62). Mr Knightley is incensed at this argument and warmly advocates the farmer's claims. But who is superior is in fact a matter of secondary consideration; what matters is Emma's cunning appeal to the notion of the gentleman. The art of defence she displays with 'rank' as a weapon is the highlight of this scene.

In a similar way Emma dexterously handles status to justify her slighting of the Bateses. Miss Bates is a favourite of everybody in Highbury except Emma, who, typically, interlinks her perverse feelings with the question of social position. Among Mr Woodhouse's acquaintances who are on visiting terms with him, Mrs and Miss Bates are classified in 'a second set', as following 'the chosen and the best' (20). It is of course Emma's view that they belong to a 'second' group, but there is something dubious about this classification. Mrs Bates, impoverished as she is now, is 'the widow of a former vicar of Highbury' (21), and there was a time, as Mr Knightley says, when Miss Bates's 'notice' was 'an honour' to Emma (375); but the Bateses are pushed into a lower class, while the incumbent vicar is placed, as we have seen, among 'the chosen and the best'. Emma's contemptuous treatment of them is not confined to this instance, and her ill feelings—especially towards Miss Bates—are closely related to her jealous rivalry with Jane Fairfax. As Nardin points out, 'it is always clear to Emma that Jane Fairfax, whom she regards as a threatening rival, holds the first place in Miss Bates's affection and esteem', and Emma cannot bear this;[7] she is irritated to see Jane Fairfax 'so idolized and so cried up . . . by her aunt and grandmother' (203). This is indeed a circumstance which highly offends Emma's sense of superiority; whence come her ill feelings towards these 'idolizers' and her reducing of them to a 'second' grade. Emma of course cannot admit this trick of reduction to herself; on the contrary, she ascribes her coldness towards them to their inferiority in social position. Emma's reluctance to go near the Bateses' house is attributed, among other things, to 'the horror of being in danger of falling in with the second rate and third rate of Highbury, who were calling on them for ever' (155). The Bateses, obviously, who enjoy the company of those callers of the 'second' and 'third rate', are ranked as their fellow creatures (indeed, they and their callers are precisely the constituents of what Emma terms 'the inferior society of Highbury' [23]), and under this 'horror' of associating with 'inferior' people is concealed her real horror—of associating with Jane Fairfax's idolizers. The Bateses' allegedly low position, together with the allegedly low company they keep, affords a pretext for Emma to justify her own 'low' passions.

Thus Emma's enthusiasm for social discrimination is inspired not so much by a snobbish instinct as by an instinct of self-justification. Indeed, when she broaches the subject of rank or position, it is a sign that she has some motives or reasons—usually not laudable ones—to cover up and disguise. She lays exaggerated emphasis on Robert Martin's humble station, not because she actually has a low opinion of farmers, but because she wants to get rid of this farmer who stands in the way of her cherished match-making project; it is a stratagem to shuffle off responsibility onto his position. When Frank Churchill proposes the revival of balls at the Crown Inn, Emma at first makes difficulties, pleading the inconvenience of 'a confusion of rank' (198); but it is an ostensible reason to conceal her real sentiment—her unwillingness to mix with those she dislikes. For Emma the social position of other people is an implement with which to camouflage her egotism—'high pillars' to misdirect herself as well as others. Moreover, this misleading implement is in itself hollow and unsubstantial, as we see in her way of dealing with Harriet and the Bateses. The status she uses as a plea is in many cases arbitrarily determined by herself. In this respect the hierarchical system of her society meets her convenience; its intricacy, plasticity, and fluidity provide a soil very favourable to her machinations. As MacDonagh remarks, a fixed social order exists only as an abstract notion; it is no exaggeration, therefore, to say that everyone has his or her own version of a fixed order. Consequently, no one—even Mr Knightley—can conclusively and convincingly refute Emma's allegations. Indeed, Emma makes dexterous, if unfair, use of the features of her society.

But, if the social order in the old society was unfixed and fluid, the leadership of the gentry in their communities was on the whole firm and indisputable, although their exalted position imposed heavy responsibilities. It was a commonly accepted idea that the gentry's privileges—such as wealth, leisure, and education—were given to them to serve the public. The English gentry, generally speaking, had a strong sense of responsibility and fulfilled 'their role as keepers of the peace, unpaid civil administrators, promoters of the public good and benefactors of the poor and unfortunate'.[8] This idea of *noblesse oblige* is also prevalent in the world of *Emma*, and how those who are in a privileged position should behave towards their inferiors is a recurrent topic in the book. Frank Churchill neglects to make a courtesy visit to his father on his marriage, for which Mr Knightley blames him, putting particular emphasis on his lack of consideration for Mrs Weston: 'It is on her account that attention to Randalls is doubly due, and she must doubly feel the omission. Had she been a person of consequence herself, he would have come I dare say; and it would not have signified whether he did or no' (149). A similar view is expressed when Mr Weston advises Frank not to defer his visit to Jane Fairfax: 'any want of attention to her *here* should be carefully avoided. You saw her with the Campbells when she was the equal of every body she mixed with, but here she is with a poor old grandmother, who has barely enough to live on. If you do not call early it will be a slight' (194). The lower a person's position or the more adverse a person's circumstances, the more attention is due—this is the principle the two gentlemen formulate, and it is a key principle in a hierarchical society. How, then, is Emma's behaviour to be understood in terms of this principle? And how is her sense of superiority interrelated with her sense of duty?

Towards the end of the novel there is a scene where Emma calls on Jane Fairfax whose engagement with Frank Churchill has been almost openly recognized, and the narrator tells us that it is 'equally as a duty and pleasure' that she makes this visit (452). This is a rare instance in Emma's career when 'duty' and 'pleasure' go hand in hand smoothly and harmoniously, for how to reconcile these two incompatible things is indeed constantly a problem for her. As a member—or, a 'mistress'—of a family who are 'first in consequence' in Highbury (7), Emma is aware that she is expected to offer gracious attentions to the underprivileged, and she believes that she understands her duty well. It is frequently the case, however, that her sense and performance of duty are distorted by the pursuit of her own pleasure. In the midst of the match-making intrigue Emma calls on a poor sick family with Harriet to give them 'relief' (86). As Nardin points out, however, Emma performs this charitable act primarily to indulge in the pleasure of feeling her own superiority. Whether the visit is really of benefit to the family is open to question.[9] Emma's 'charity' is in fact a pleasure enjoyed in the name of duty, and so is her attempt at match-making for Harriet. When she decides to 'notice' her, she regards it not only as 'a very kind undertaking' but also as 'highly becoming her own situation in life, her leisure, and powers' (24). Her officious patronage of Harriet allows her to indulge in the pleasure of feeling superior; she defines it as a duty, but it is an invented duty that is superfluous and even pernicious. In her 'real' duties, on the other hand, she is often negligent, as is implied in the dissatisfaction Mr Knightley expresses every now and then in regard to her lack of consideration for Jane Fairfax and the Bateses. The cause of her negligence is that she derives no pleasure in discharging such duties.

Yet Emma is by no means always negligent or wrong-headedly assiduous; she can be rational and considerate sometimes, and especially within her own family circle she conscientiously discharges her duties even at the sacrifice of her personal pleasure. The thoughtful attention she shows to Mr Woodhouse is a good example; she is unremittingly careful of his comfort, spares no pains to humour his gentle selfishness, and is always ready to comply with the requests of a fastidious and valetudinarian father. She is an exemplary dutiful daughter. In the scenes of family gatherings she plays the role of a vigilant peace watcher. Mr John Knightley, somewhat intolerant and short-tempered, occasionally provokes Emma or agitates her father by his sarcasm or acerbity. Emma, however, taking it upon herself to 'keep the peace if possible' (97), never lets her feelings run away with her on such occasions and, when in a fit of ill humour he darkens the atmosphere, tries sedulously to restore the harmony. Within her own family circle Emma's sense of duty is sound, and her personal pleasure is always subordinated to the performance of her duties. It is when she steps into the outside world that this order of priority is completely reversed; there pleasure obtrudes itself as the primary motivation of Emma's actions, and her sense of duty is either muffled into silence or warped into a corrupt form. In *Amelia* Henry Fielding observes through the voice of Dr Harrison that 'whoever discharges his Duty well' to blood relations 'gives us a well-grounded Hope, that he will behave as properly in all the rest'.[10] But Fielding's proposition, sound as it may be as a generalization, does not apply in Emma's case.

Why, then, does Emma's behaviour inside and outside the family circle differ so radically? One may find an explanation in the difference in stability of Emma's own position. Within her family circle, Emma's status as the 'first' person is firmly established. With her father she is always first—first in affection and esteem—and she herself confidently says: 'I believe few married women are half as much mistress of their husband's house, as I am of Hartfield' (84). There is actually no one in the family circle—including the sober and unflattering Knightley brothers—who dares to call her position into question or attempt to supplant her. She is of the first importance in her family. In the outside world, however, her premiership is by no means so firm or unchallenged. There appear rivals one after another who, intentionally or unintentionally, present a threat to her foremost position: Jane Fairfax surpasses Emma in accomplishments; the Coles aggrandize themselves at an alarming rate; and Mrs Elton contests with her for leadership in the village. Emma of course cannot bring herself to accept a subordinate position. She is deeply disconcerted when Mrs Weston suggests the possibility of Mr Knightley's being in love with Jane Fairfax, because, apart from her subconscious affection for Mr Knightley, she cannot bear the idea of Jane Fairfax's becoming '[a] Mrs. Knightley for them all to give way to' (228). But in reality she is more than once obliged to 'give way'. At the ball in the Crown Inn 'Emma must submit to stand second to Mrs Elton', and, as the narrator ironically adds, 'It was almost enough to make her think of marrying' (325). In the outside world where her position is often threatened, she is impelled to do what is unnecessary in the family circle—to flaunt her superiority. When she first proposes the theory that Harriet is a gentleman's daughter, she advises Harriet: 'you must support your claim to that station by every thing within your own power, or there will be plenty of people who would take pleasure in degrading you' (30). It is not Harriet, however, but Emma herself who faithfully follows this advice; to support her claim to the first position she takes every pain to show off her superiority, 'or there will be plenty of people who would take pleasure in degrading' her. And, in fact, to show off and feel her own superiority is a pleasure to her.

In pursuit of this pleasure she sometimes fabricates superfluous duties, and sometimes neglects to perform her real ones. In both cases she resorts to her characteristic far-fetched rationalization, and in both cases her conduct threatens to deflect or disrupt the village life. To show off her superiority she meddlesomely patronizes Harriet. She thinks she is doing her duty, but thanks to this extra 'duty' Harriet loses her way, severed from an environment congenial to her. In her dereliction of duty Emma poses an even more serious threat, and her rationalization there is more glaringly contradictory. In the small society of Highbury she avoids contact as much as possible with those whose company does not gratify her sense of superiority, and so she seldom goes near the Bateses' house. As we have seen, to excuse her negligence she pleads their low social position. But this method of self-justification carries an obvious paradox. Emma, who takes pride in her high social position, also takes pride in fulfilling those duties which appertain to her high position, and she knows that the first duty of her position is to be a kind friend to the underprivileged. And yet, where the fulfilment of this duty does not minister to her sense of superiority, she evades it by alleging the social inferiority of those to whom she ought to be kind, and this inferiority is mostly of her own invention. It is natural that such a self-contradictory pattern of behaviour should give itself away, and this happens when Emma is unable to avoid contact with Miss Bates; during the excursion to Box Hill, she holds up Miss Bates to public ridicule. This act—a grave transgression against the principle of patronage in a hierarchy—is not an inadvertent act committed on the spur of the moment; fundamental flaws lurking in her daily conduct manifest themselves in the nasty form of cruel derision. Indeed, this incident exposes the gross paradox involved in Emma's cunning exploitation of the flexibility of her society, and her flagrant offence signals how her frantic superiority-hunting menaces the delicate equilibrium maintained in that flexible social system.

❦

Let us finally consider the peculiar idiosyncrasies of the heroine of the novel in the historical context and explore the author's intention in delineating them. Emma's superiority complex, as we may call it, has a close relationship to the fact that the Woodhouses are not a landowning family. They derive their income not from land but from 'other sources'—presumably from investment. From the statement that they are 'the younger branch of a very ancient family', we may assume that the progenitor of the Hartfield Woodhouses was a younger brother in a landed family, who entered trade, made his fortune, purchased the Hartfield estate (from the Knightleys, no doubt), and settled in Highbury (or, the purchase may have been effected by the next generation, as with the Bingleys in *Pride and Prejudice*). It is clear, therefore—as it was no doubt clear to the contemporary reader—that, although they have settled in Highbury 'for several generations' and are now admitted to be 'first in consequence' there, the Woodhouses in fact stand in almost the same position as the Westons, the Coles, and the Sucklings of Maple Grove. These are all nonlanded rentier families, and the marked increase of such *nouveaux riches* was a distinct characteristic of the society of Jane Austen's days. Claire Tomalin's biography reveals that the society in which the Austen family moved in Hampshire was by no means an unchanging, orderly rural world, as one would expect, but was a restless fluid world, filled with those who 'were what has been called in this century pseudo-gentry, families who aspired to live by the values of the gentry without owning land or inherited wealth of any significance'.[11] David Spring, one of the earliest to apply the term 'pseudo-gentry' to this group, remarks of the behaviour of those aspirants and the influence they had on their society:

> they had a sharp eye for the social escalators, were skilled in getting on them, and (what was more important) no less skilled in staying on them. They were adept at acquiring what the economist Fred

Hirsch has aptly called 'positional goods'—those scarce services, jobs, and goods which announce social success. In this they helped to inaugurate a 'positional competition' inevitably more widespread than that indulged in by landowners....[12]

As a member of a parvenu family of comparative seniority, Emma struggles to stay on the social escalators, but she goes a little too far; intent upon outdoing her rivals, she becomes obsessed with monopolizing the 'positional goods'. Indeed, Emma's morbid desire for superiority is an unhealthy symptom of the 'positional competition' which was spurred on by the rapid rise of a new social force.

Was it, then, Jane Austen's intention to criticize the newly emerging gentry? The Woodhouses' nonlanded status is emphasized by several critics as the main cause of Emma's inadequate understanding of her duties. Nardin observes that, in contrast to Mr Knightley, the landed squire of Highbury, the Woodhouses, though they reside there, 'lack the sort of natural, historic ties to the place and its people which land ownership provides for Mr Knightley', and this lack of real ties, according to Nardin, prevents Emma from cultivating a proper sense of what is due to the inhabitants.[13] Beth Fowkes Tobin develops this argument further and propounds the view that by 'idealizing the landlord and criticizing the monied status of the new gentry' Jane Austen attempted to fend off attacks being delivered from several quarters against the landowning classes and thus to advocate the traditional paternalistic system based on land ownership; Emma's moral inadequacies are highlighted in order to lay the blame on the nonlanded new gentry.[14] The 'idealized landlord' is of course Mr Knightley, and there certainly is no objection to seeing him as an exemplary landowner. It is also undeniable that Emma's deficiencies are in many ways linked to her 'monied status'. But did Jane Austen really attempt such defence? Given the elaborate and highly systematized description of those deficiencies, one can hardly suppose that Jane Austen's purpose was simply to vindicate one group or class or to blame another; her penetration into the depths of Emma's consciousness even suggests a scientific attitude of mind free from any political bias. What, then, was she doing in this novel?

Fully aware of the rapid growth of the new type of gentry in this period, Jane Austen was also aware that, with their proliferation, a certain ethos—a sort of competitive atmosphere—had become prevalent in society. That she took a keen interest in the matter is obvious, not only from her portrayal in this novel of a heroine obsessed with superiority, but also from her introduction of a caricature of the heroine—Mrs Elton. Mrs Elton is herself a daughter of a Bristol merchant of 'moderate' dignity (183), but she has a more prosperous brother-in-law, Mr Suckling, whose family has been successful enough to purchase an estate, Maple Grove. With this typical parvenu of a brother-in-law and his 'seat' as her tower of strength, Mrs Elton enters Highbury, meaning 'to shine and be very superior' (272). Indeed, 'extremely well satisfied with herself, and thinking much of her importance' (272), Mrs Elton reiterates many of Emma's own conceited words and deeds. Emma's superiority complex, as manifested in her overweening social pretensions, self-righteous patronage, or petty rivalries, is in an exaggerated way reproduced in this character. Concerning the role of Mrs Elton, Alistair Duckworth observes that 'Jane Austen's intention is clearly to repeat certain of Emma's characteristics in a manifestly inferior personality and thus to expose them'.[15] But what are exposed are more than Emma's personal defects; if 'certain of Emma's characteristics' reflect a particular tendency of this period, then the author's intention in parodying them in another character is evidently to 'expose' and accentuate the tendency. It is a clever device to indicate that Emma's superiority complex is not just the problem of one individual alone.

But this does not necessarily point to a hostile or aggressive intent of the author against the parvenu gentry; nor was her object in the book merely to lay bare the obnoxiousness of the *arriviste* qualities they possessed. She underlined the cult of arrivism because it was closely related to an alarming phenomenon in her society—the derangement of the hierarchical system. As a keen observer of society, she perceived the traditional framework of society and the way of life within it seriously dislocated with the rapid growth of the new social force; with their powerful ambition and vigorous spirit of emulation, those climbers of the social ladder distorted the order and principle of that ladder, the hierarchy. Her main concern in the novel was to carry out a close inspection of this phenomenon. In view of her acute psychological insight into the matter, however, unclouded by emotional involvement but marked by a spirit of detachment, denunciation of the newly risen class or advocacy of the particular social system of the age seems to have formed little part of her plan. Mark Parker remarks that recent Austen criticism, in exploring the political dimension of her novels, 'has grappled with the problem of how to attach a context (drawn from a pool of possible contexts) to Austen's novels in the absence of some of the more direct signs of political affiliation and tendency'.[16] Yet this 'absence' of the 'direct signs of political affiliation and tendency' could be regarded as the very sign of Jane Austen's unwillingness to commit herself to a particular political position.

What, then, did she aim at in her inquiry into the phenomenon? Perhaps one could put it this way: well aware of the inevitability of hierarchy in human society, Jane Austen directed her attention to its immutable and enduring, rather than topical and transitory, aspects, and her ultimate object in her inspection of the matter was to elucidate the way hierarchy would function—or, more correctly, the way it would malfunction. To put it another way, the complication of the hierarchical system afforded her an excellent opportunity for studying this problem, and among the factors of the complication what engaged her interest most was the behaviour of the disturbers. The superiority complex which an upstart was prone to, and the self-deception previously examined in several characters, which she knew could easily be united with a superiority complex—these she regarded as essential ingredients of a malfunctioning social hierarchy. Perhaps, while engaged in *Mansfield Park*, she already cherished a design to handle the theme of self-deception on a yet larger scale in future. If so, this design, when she actually put her hand to a new work, entered into happy combination with the task she assigned to herself in it—to illustrate the psychological mechanism of abnormal functioning incident to a system of hierarchy. And, given the masterly delineation of Emma's subtle ways of abusing rank and position, we can say that Jane Austen superbly accomplished her purpose.

CHAPTER 6

An Organization that Works:
Persuasion

With the unfinished *Sanditon* excepted, *Persuasion* stands last in Jane Austen's novels, and it is often argued that the author tried to explore something new in this last work. Its heroine is the twenty-seven-year-old Anne Elliot, who 'had been forced into prudence in her youth', but 'learned romance as she grew older' (30). Apparently Anne takes a reverse course to that which her predecessors have followed, and besides this instance of the heroine, the novel has some such aspects as seem to depart from the beaten path. For these renovative elements *Persuasion* is sometimes compared to *The Tempest*, 'another final work that reprises and transforms themes and motifs introduced earlier in the author's canon'.[1] Indeed, the ways the novelist 'transformed' have been discussed from various points of view, and among the noticeable new elements in the book what seems to draw critical attention most is the apparent change in the author's attitude towards the established order. In the previous works Jane Austen's faith in the traditional framework of society seems to be firm or even implicit, but in *Persuasion* she loses that faith, depicting the decline of the gentry, the admitted pillar of that framework—this, roughly speaking, is the gist of the argument widely prevalent in the latter half of the twentieth century. The 'decline' of the gentry began to be spoken of in the 1950s, and in the 70s and 80s, when critics became more and more alert to the links between the actual and fictional worlds, many of them came to consider that the shift in Jane Austen's position reflects the actual changes that were going on in the society of this period. Tony Tanner is one of them. He perceives in the novelist a 'transfer of allegiance and emotional investment from the English ruling classes . . . to the navy'. About the social situation of this time he remarks thus: 'The novel shows that English society is . . . "in between": in between an old social order in a state of decline and desuetude, and some new "modern" society of as yet uncertain values, hierarchies and principles'. And because of this fluxing state of society, Tanner considers the 'transfer of allegiance' in Jane Austen 'doubly understandable'.[2] That some sorts of social changes were happening in this time is certainly undeniable, yet a certain doubt remains: did Jane Austen's attitude really so radically change as this kind of argument implies?

The appearance of defection on the side of the author is of course due to her way of representing Sir Walter Elliot, who is without doubt a figure the most unfavourably drawn of all the landlords that appear in the novels. Sir Walter's character is at once established at the outset of the book, which opens with a picture of the baronet addicted to the Baronetage. He is a man 'delighted with the place he held in society' (4), and is 'a conceited, silly father' (5); moreover, he has incurred heavy debts by his extravagance, which eventually obliges him to rent out and leave his ancestral estate. The opening chapters indeed bring into relief Sir Walter's sheer lack of qualifications as a landholder; but we should be careful in linking this portrait of the baronet to something like general 'decline' of the gentry in this period. Taking issue with those critics who have read a downward trend of the gentry in the novels and laying stress on the prosperous condition English landowners were then in, David Spring remarks thus: 'Oblivious to landowners' political power and progressive economics, some interpreters of Jane Austen have seen weakness and crisis and change in landed fortunes, where they should instead have seen strength and stability and continuity'. As for Sir Walter's letting out of Kellynch Hall, which has often been seen as 'a portent of the imminent downfall of landed society', Spring categorizes it as no more than 'an ancient expedient for debt-ridden landowners'.[3] As we shall see later, Spring's assertion is quite true—the gentry in Jane Austen's time were by no means in decline. If, then, the actual state of affairs of this period belies those interpretations of 'decline', how should we read such a negative portrayal of a landholder, and, for that matter, how should we view the navy officers who seem to be given such enthusiastic endorsement of the author, and who are often seen as a symbol of a rising new power that would be replacing the declining old one? Given the increasing trend in recent Austen criticism towards a cultural contextualizing of her novels, these questions are worth considering anew, and to grasp the full meaning of the contrast between the gentry and the navy, it is necessary first to examine carefully the lifestyle of the baronet and his family.

In the opening chapter the narrator remarks: 'Vanity was the beginning and the end of Sir Walter Elliot's character; vanity of person and of situation' (4). Indeed, Sir Walter is a man whose mind is occupied solely with external things such as personal appearance and social position, and, with Anne excepted, this obsession with mere facades of life—social position, especially—is a predominant feature of the Elliot family. They are inordinately proud of their stations and extremely jealous of their places in society. When Admiral Croft turns up as a candidate for his tenant, Sir Walter feels satisfied with his 'situation in life, which was just high enough, and not too high'. He reasons thus: 'An admiral speaks his own consequence, and, at the same time, can never make a baronet look small. In all their dealings and intercourse, Sir Walter Elliot must ever have the precedence' (24). His two daughters are of the same vein. The eldest one Elizabeth is 'in the habit of . . . general observance as "Miss Elliot" (147), and on ceremonial occasions always occupies a leading place as her due. Indeed, as Anne admits, 'Elizabeth must be first' (147). Her sister Mary, on the other hand, is not faring so well in the Musgrove family. She complains to Anne that 'Mrs. Musgrove was very apt not to give her the precedence that was her due' (45–46). Her pride in her baronet blood is such that, when Anne comes to her house, she insists that the people of the Great House should first pay a courtesy visit to *her* sister instead of her calling on them.

Such preoccupation with rank and status was perhaps not quite uncommon. Concerning the pride of the gentry in those days G. E. Mingay observes thus:

> It is true that the gentry's belief in their inherent superiority and

natural right to regulate the 'lower orders' led sometimes to overbearing pride and misuse of the extensive powers they commanded. Inevitably they also expected an unceasing tribute of deference from the inferiors whose lives they influenced at every turn. Their sensitive sense of status exhibited itself even in disputes over the ranking of private family pews in the most prominent part of the church.

So far Mingay's observation is an apt description of the Elliot family, but what follows does not apply to them at all:

> Nevertheless, it is remarkable that the English gentry in general showed a strong sense of public duty and of social obligation towards their subordinates.[4]

Indeed, this consciousness of *noblesse oblige* is totally absent in Sir Walter and his eldest daughter's minds. They are indifferent to their subordinates and, apparently, it is Anne alone in the family who practices such acts of patronage as charity (she continues her charity visits after they move to Bath).[5] Her sister Elizabeth has 'no habits of utility abroad', and when informed of their financial embarrassments, one of the plans of economy she proposes is 'to cut off some unnecessary charities' (9). Naturally enough, they enjoy little popularity among the tenantry and cottagers; at their departure for Bath the Elliots are seen off only by those 'who might have had a hint to shew themselves' (36). Later, when the Crofts have occupied Kellynch Hall for some time, Anne feels that the change of residents turns out to be beneficial:

> she had in fact so high an opinion of the Crofts, and considered her father so very fortunate in his tenants, felt the parish to be so sure of a good example, and the poor of the best attention and relief, that however sorry and ashamed for the necessity of the removal, she could not but in conscience feel that they were gone who deserved not to stay, and that Kellynch-hall had passed into better

hands than its owners'. (125)

And then, when she comes to Bath to find her father and sister thoroughly satisfied with their new house in Camden-place, 'she must sigh that her father should feel no degradation in his change; should see nothing to regret in the duties and dignity of the resident land-holder' (138). Sir Walter stands at the top of the local hierarchy, but with such dereliction on the part of its leader, the system of the hierarchy has fallen into serious dysfunction.

Just as the social position of Sir Walter and Elizabeth is dissociated from the roles which ought to accompany it, so are their manners void of their important function. In *Mansfield Park* Edmund Bertram urges on Mary Crawford the importance of a clergyman's manners as an example to his parishioners (Vol. I Ch. IX), and of course his argument applies to the gentry, the leaders of local communities. Citing Edmund Burke's discourse upon the moral influence of manners, David Monaghan points out the crucial role of manners of the local landowner:

> more important than any act of patronage were the ritual means by which he could express an awareness of the needs of others. . . . Not even the most influential of landowners could actively demonstrate his concern for others as often and in as many different situations as was possible through polite behaviour.[6]

Needless to say, it requires inner sound morality for manners to have such influence. Meeting him at Bath, Lady Russell is at once prepossessed by Mr Elliot's manners, convinced of 'the solid so fully supporting the superficial' (146); but her judgement proves wrong—there are no 'correct opinions and well regulated mind' beneath the 'general politeness and suavity' of his manners (249). In a similar way, neither Sir Walter nor Elizabeth, though their manners could be 'a model of good breeding' (32), has this inner support. Their manners are just a tool to keep up the dignity of their social position, and they do not even function as a lubricant in daily social intercourses. When Sir Walter and Elizabeth present themselves at the hotel where the Musgroves stay,

> Anne felt an instant oppression, and, wherever she looked, saw symptoms of the same. The comfort, the freedom, the gaiety of the room was over, hushed into cold composure, determined silence, or insipid talk, to meet the heartless elegance of her father and sister. (226)

Their manners, which cannot even lubricate ordinary social intercourses, cannot have the moral influence that Burke made so much of. And here is another sign of a gulf between leaders and their inferiors—a sign that the hierarchy does not work.

This atrophy of the system of hierarchy is subtly hinted in the representation of the social world of Bath. Owing to the increase of popularity as a fashionable resort, the city area of Bath extended rapidly from the latter half of the eighteenth century and, along with this extension, the importance of a good address increased, especially for such pretentious visitors and residents as Sir Walter Elliot. From the old town the residential quarters grew northward and uphill, and, as Keiko Parker shows, the level of habitation rises as the ground ascends.[7] Camden-place where Sir Walter so glories in locating himself was in those days 'nearly the northernmost point of the city, in other words, at nearly the *highest* point of its elevation',[8] and Lady Russell, 'the widow of only a knight' (11), takes her lodgings in Rivers-street, southward of Camden-place and a little lower. Gay-street where the Crofts takes their lodgings is still further down, but not so down as to be unfashionable—they place themselves 'perfectly to Sir Walter's satisfaction' (168). Westgate Buildings where the impoverished Mrs Smith lives, on the other hand, are located at the low end of the city and is held in undisguised contempt by Sir Walter. Thus the characters, including such marginal ones as Lady Dalrymple and Colonel Wallis who are also given appropriate addresses in Laura-place and Marlborough Buildings respectively, are situated rigorously according to their social ranks, and this mechanically arranged inorganic hierarchy in a leading resort of the country implies its general trend; as Parker aptly observes, 'the whole of Bath is revealed as a metaphor for society at large'.[9]

❦

The Elliots' way of life, which gives every sign of malfunction in the traditional system of hierarchy, is contrasted in this novel with lifestyles of other groups of people, and one of them is the Musgroves of Uppercross. The family of Uppercross Cottage where Anne stays hold daily intercourse with that of the Great House, and the bustling and unceremonious communal life they lead together presents a striking contrast to 'the sameness and the elegance, the prosperity and the nothingness' of everyday life at Kellynch Hall (9). Yet Anne is by no means better off at Uppercross. In her home at Kellynch, with all her 'elegance of mind and sweetness of character', she is 'nobody with either father or sister' (5), and at Uppercross her merits are likewise scarcely appreciated. Moreover, at the Great House as well as at the Cottage she is 'treated with too much confidence by all parties' and is 'too much in the secret of the complaints of each house' (44). Indeed, Anne is pestered from all sides with their grumbles against each other, and such a role of a repository of complaints becomes a considerable burden to her. It is worth noting here that this position of Anne at Uppercross bears a close resemblance to that of Fanny Price during the theatrical episode in *Mansfield Park*. Mansfield Park is a place governed by a strict code of decorum, but once the theatrical scheme is set in motion, the young 'actors' are placed 'on a footing which must do away all restraints' with one another (*MP* 154), and this disappearance of 'restraints'—the code of manners, that is—brings out their latent ugliness: 'So far from being all satisfied and all enjoying ... every body [was] requiring something they had not, and giving occasion of discontent to the others', and 'Fanny, being always a very courteous listener, and often the only listener at hand, came in for the complaints and distresses of most of them' (*MP* 164–65). Thus Mansfield falls into a state of moral anarchy, with unleashed egoism crashing everywhere, and in a similar, though milder, way the world of Uppercross is filled with an 'air of confusion' (40).

In *Mansfield Park* an important factor that caused the moral anarchy is the strict formality which reigns in the Bertram household; the acting scheme is in a sense an inevitable reaction against too rigid control, and, as we have examined in Chapter 4, this picture of control and reaction has a close relationship to the social background of the period. In the reactionary atmosphere of the 1790s there grew up an urgent call for reform of manners and morals, and led by ardent and energetic reformers, the Evangelicals, active campaigns for moral improvement got under way. This widespread movement eventually made a profound impact on the national life; around the turn of the century public opinion became powerfully in favour of strict morals. But this rapid shift in the social atmosphere had its negative side. For one thing, what appeared to be an improvement in morals was often a mere patching up of facades, as Jane Austen subtly exposes in *Mansfield Park*, and if Sir Thomas Bertram is an embodiment of a hypocritical aspect of the new ethos produced by the reform movement, Sir Walter Elliot is a grotesque caricature of it—a dried-up specimen of the reformed manners. For another, the movement, commanding and forcible in its operations, provoked a fierce reaction in some quarters, and the Regency period is characterized by the prevalence of a sort of desperate dissipation amid the marked conversion to a moralistic society. The Musgroves' free and somewhat tumultuous life could be regarded as a version of this trend, and, if the anarchy in the theatrical episode is caused by a reaction against the rigid control of Sir Thomas, the confusion which reigns in the world of Uppercross is caused, in part at least, by their reaction against the lifestyle of the Elliots. Louisa Musgrove is severely critical about her sister-in-law's obstinate adherence to 'place' and 'rank', deprecatingly calling it 'the Elliot pride' (88), and, indeed, the Musgroves are noticeably indifferent to these kinds of ceremonious aspects of life. There is no stiff formality in the intercourse between the families of the Great House and the Cottage, who are 'in the habit of running in and out of each other's house at all hours' (36); and except for Mary, the Musgroves, who are 'in the first class of society in the country', show no contempt for the Hayters, who 'would . . . have been hardly in any class at all, but for their connexion with Uppercross' (74). As we have seen, however, in this unceremonious way of life 'there were on each side continual subjects of offence' (40). The warm friendliness of the Musgroves is certainly more appealing than the cold elegance of the Elliots, but too much informality has inevitably its own drawbacks.

The friendliness which marks the life of the Musgroves is also a conspicuous feature of another group of people appearing in this novel—the naval officers and their families. Admiral and Mrs Croft, when they settle in Kellynch, are quite amicable to their new neighbours, the Musgroves and Lady Russell, as well as to Anne, and at Lyme Regis the party from Uppercross are deeply affected by the cordial reception of the Harvilles, whose hospitality is 'so uncommon, so unlike the usual style of give-and-take invitations, and dinners of formality and display' (98). When the party have left their house, Louisa Musgrove who has been already biased in favour of the navy 'burst forth into raptures of admiration and delight on the character of the navy—their friendliness, their brotherliness, their openness, their uprightness' (99). But what is also notable about them is that their life is highly functional, quite free either from the formal showiness of the Elliots or from the 'confusion' of the Musgroves. After moving to Kellynch Hall, the Crofts make several alterations to the house, which include removing looking-glasses, mending the laundry-door, and placing umbrellas near at hand. The large looking-glasses which abounded in the dressing-room are remnants of Sir Walter's personal vanity and the Admiral prefers his 'little shaving glass in one corner' (128). As for the laundry-door which was left unrepaired, Roger Sales surmises that this 'was probably in a part of the house that Sir Walter felt it was beneath his dignity to visit'.[10] Umbrellas were formerly kept in the butler's room, which 'underlines Sir Walter's need to be served, even at the cost of common sense and his own convenience'.[11] Indeed, these changes bespeak the Crofts' preference of practicability and functionality over ostentation and dignity. In respect of functionality, however, a more impressive instance is afforded by the way Captain Harville manages his household. The house to which he invites the party from Uppercross is so small that Anne has 'a moment's astonishment'; but

> it was soon lost in the pleasanter feelings which sprang from the

> sight of all the ingenious contrivances and nice arrangements of Captain Harville, to turn the actual space to the best possible account, to supply the deficiencies of lodging-house furniture, and defend the windows and doors against the winter storms to be expected. (98)

These neat and utilitarian habits of the sailors, fostered no doubt from their professional life, are obviously meant to form a contrast to the sterile elegant life of the Elliots, but there is more to the matter. Their profession itself conjures up a significant image against the contemporary system of hierarchy which fell into a serious malfunction.

The sailors in this novel have of course received constant critical attention, and hitherto they have often been seen as people altogether different from the gentry. Indeed, there seems to be a fixed image in our mind concerning the respective social standings of the gentry and the sailors—that the former belong to a landowning class with their hereditary estates, and the latter to a professional class, gaining their status and fortunes by their own abilities and efforts. Perhaps no one is so sensitive to the difference between the two groups as Sir Walter Elliot. When Mr Shepherd recommends a naval officer for a tenant of Kellynch Hall, Sir Walter cavils at the profession, describing it disdainfully as a 'means of bringing persons of obscure birth into undue distinction, and raising men to honours which their fathers and grandfathers never dreamt of'. He goes on to illustrate his point and refers to one Lord St Ives, 'whose father we all know to have been a country curate, without bread to eat'; but he 'was to give place to Lord St. Ives' (19–20). Yet things were in fact not so bad as Sir Walter represents them. Based on the two biographical works on the Navy officers in those days, John Marshall's *Royal Naval Biography* (1825) and William O'Byrne's *A Naval Biographical Dictionary* (1849), Michael Lewis draws up a table of social status of the Navy officers' parents during the years 1793–1815, and according to this table the officers whose parents were landowners account for nearly 40 % of the total number.[12] As Lewis emphasizes, there are inadequacies of various kinds in the two materials, but he admits that 'our tally from both authorities ... seems to show that

British landowners (and particularly their younger sons) were playing a conspicuous part in the sea-defence of Britain'.[13] At the same time, there were undeniably many officers whose parents belonged to lower social groups, and the table shows that the officers account for 50 % whose parents were 'professional men'—people in such lines of work as the Navy itself, the Army, the Church, the Law, and Medicine. Some of these comparatively low-born men actually ascended to great honours, a typical example of which is Horatio Nelson, whose father was a country clergyman, but who, apart from his early successive promotions in the Navy, was first invested with the Order of the Bath, then made Baron Nelson of the Nile, and finally created Viscount Nelson. In *Persuasion* Captain Wentworth, whose unspecified parentage is certainly not high, has similarly achieved early promotions in his profession and acquired a considerable fortune by his own energy. In our image the sailors who thus live in a world of meritocracy tend to be categorized into a vigorous 'new' power as opposed to the decadent old power, the gentry. But such views seem to obscure an important message tacitly woven into the novel. In order to decipher this covert message, we need to see the Navy as an organization in a somewhat different light.

The world of the Royal Navy could be described as a world of strict hierarchy, with the Admiralty at its head and its commissioned officers ranked in orderly rows from Admiral to Lieutenant. This hierarchy of officers—'the naval hierarchy', as Lewis calls it—was not exactly a hierarchy within a ship of war. Admirals, including vice-admirals and rear-admirals, were not in command of a single ship but were flag officers in a fleet, a number of warships acting together, and it was captains that took command of each ship, within which was formed its own hierarchy.[14] As a head of this 'ship hierarchy' a captain was required to possess considerable ability in management. Brian Lavery describes the various aspects of ship administration thus:

> A large ship of war was a cross-section of society, except that few, if any, women and young children were on board when at sea. A captain could call on the resources of many different experts—the

seamen, petty officers, master and lieutenants who made the ship mobile; the medical team under the surgeon; skilled craftsmen such as the carpenter and his crew, the caulkers, coopers, armourers, tailors, and sailmakers; intellectuals like the chaplain and schoolmaster; a unit of disciplined soldiers under the officers of marines; clerical and administrative staff such as the purser and captain's clerk; and experienced artillerymen under the gunner and his mates. A ship could be free of the shore for up to three months at a time, and independent of the naval supply organisation for longer than that, if the captain was able to find water and food on his own initiative. Its men had to be fed and paid, reports had to be made to the Admiralty and to the commander of the fleet, and logs and journals written up.[15]

A ship of war was indeed a community in which each member had his role to fulfil, and Lavery emphasizes the need for organization to enable this seafaring community to work efficiently:

A first rate ship had a crew of over 800 men, and even a large frigate had nearly 300. Many of these were disaffected, unwilling, illiterate or stupid. From time to time, most of them could be disgruntled, homesick, tired, drunk or sick. But all the complex and highly-skilled manoeuvres of the ship had to be carried out. The sailors might spend years at a time on board, relying on the navy for all their material needs. They had to live together in incredibly confined space. To make such a body of men into an efficient team required an enormous degree of discipline and organisation.[16]

What is indeed remarkable is that, generally speaking, captains and other officers in Nelson's navy were very efficient and the system of the ship hierarchy functioned extremely well, which resulted in glorious victories in the Campaign of Trafalgar and other crucial engagements.

Unlike Mrs Croft, Jane Austen herself never went to sea nor experienced a life on board a ship of war; but she had two sailor brothers on active service, Francis and Charles, from whom she no doubt obtained detailed information about shipboard life. Citing the scene of the evening party where Wentworth and the Crofts entertain the Musgrove family with their anecdotes (Vol. I Ch. VIII), J. H. and E. C. Hubback observe thus:

> One cannot but feel, when one comes on such a conversation in Jane Austen's novel, how perfectly she understood the details of her brothers' lives. Her interest and sympathy were so great that we can almost hear Francis and Charles recounting experiences to their home circle, with a delicious dwelling on the dangers, for the sake of inward shudders, or 'more open exclamations of pity and horror' from their hearers, with sidelong hits at the Admiralty, and with the true sailor's love of, and pride in, the vessels he has commanded.[17]

But her knowledge went further than such items as 'the manner of living on board, daily regulations, food, hours, &c.' (64). As Brian Southam shows in detail, she was versed in the organization and machinery of the Navy,[18] and since she explored the problem of the necessary qualifications for a community leader in her previous work, *Emma*, it seems only natural that she should take an active interest in the role of naval leaders—especially captains in command of warships, amongst whom were included her own brothers (Francis was made a captain in 1800, and Charles in 1810).

As we have seen, a captain's responsibility was indeed grave; lives of the whole crew as well as success in a mission depended on his hand. To preserve discipline in ships harsh punishment was not infrequently resorted to, but of course severity alone would not go far enough;[19] sympathy and consideration to his subordinates were key requisites of a competent captain. Jane Austen certainly had this on her mind when she launched upon *Persuasion*, and, although she did not draw Wentworth (and other captains) on actual duty on board warships, several episodes—especially that of Dick Musgrove—convey that Wentworth was not just a 'dashing' sailor but a kind and considerate commander. Dick Musgrove, being 'stupid and unmanageable' (50), was one of those midshipmen whom 'every captain wishes to get rid of' (51), and, as Anne surmises, Wentworth himself 'had probably been at some pains to get rid of him' (67). But he was certainly not harsh with this unpromising midshipman. Dick was six months on board Captain Wentworth's frigate, the *Laconia*, and 'from the Laconia he had, under the influence of his captain, written the only two letters which his father and mother had ever received from him during the whole of his absence' (51). Wentworth not only encouraged Dick to write home but also was mindful of his study, which could be inferred from the phrase Dick used in his letter about his captain, 'only two perticular about the school-master' (52).

The episode of Dick Musgrove reminds one of passages in Robert Southey's *Life of Nelson*. In recording Nelson's early career Southey observes: 'His ship was full of young midshipmen, of whom there were not less than thirty on board; and happy were they whose lot it was to be placed with such a captain. . . . Every day he went into the schoolroom, to see that they were pursuing their nautical studies'. And in another place Southey writes: 'To his midshipmen he ever showed the most winning kindness, encouraging the diffident, tempering the hasty, counselling and befriending both. "Recollect," he used to say, "that you must be a seaman to be an officer; and also, that you cannot be a good officer without being a gentleman"'.[20] Indeed, Wentworth might have said these words to, say, a William Price, if not to Dick Musgrove. In her letter to Cassandra of 11 October 1813, Jane Austen says: 'Southey's Life of Nelson;—I am tired of Lives of Nelson, being that I never read any. I will read this however, if Frank is mentioned in it'.[21] In fact Frank is not mentioned, but it seems nevertheless certain that Jane Austen read this book. In her painstaking monograph on *Persuasion,* Jocelyn Harris asserts: 'Although she denied reading any lives of Nelson, she models Captain Wentworth in *Persuasion* not only on her brothers, as is well known, but also on England's foremost naval hero, especially as Robert Southey represented him in his hagiographic *Life*, printed by Austen's publisher John Murray in 1813'.[22] Of course Wentworth's career did not exactly overlap with that of Nelson, but the image of the great commander was undoubtedly projected on the fictional young captain, and Jane Austen must have been indebted to

Southey's *Life* for that image.

Nelson as Southey depicts him is indeed appealing, and what Southey repeatedly stresses is the power Nelson possessed to engage the minds of his men. 'Wherever Nelson commanded,' he writes, 'the men soon became attached to him. In ten days' time he would have restored the most mutinous ship in the navy to order'.[23] Francis Austen also applauds Nelson's consummate commanding ability. On Nelson's death at Trafalgar, he wrote to his fiancée Mary Gibson: 'I never heard of his equal, nor do I expect again to see such a man. To the soundest judgment he united prompt decision and speedy execution of his plans; and he possessed in a superior degree the happy talent of making every class of persons pleased with their situation and eager to exert themselves in forwarding the public service'.[24] And this superb leadership of Nelson Southey attributes to 'that generous regard for the feelings as well as interests of all who were under his command, which made him as much beloved in the fleets of Britain, as he was dreaded in those of the enemy'. He continues:

> Never was any commander more beloved. He governed men by their reason and their affections. They knew that he was incapable of caprice or tyranny; and they obeyed him with alacrity and joy, because he possessed their confidence as well as their love. . . . Severe discipline he detested. . . . In his whole life Nelson was never known to act unkindly towards an officer. . . . But in Nelson there was more than the easiness and humanity of a happy nature. He did not merely abstain from injury; his was an active and watchful benevolence, ever desirous not only to render justice, but to do good.[25]

This 'active and watchful benevolence' of Nelson is shared by Captain Wentworth. Captain Benwick—this 'captain' is a courtesy title; his real rank is commander—was once First Lieutenant of the *Laconia*; that is, he was an aide-de-camp of Wentworth. He was engaged to Captain Harville's sister, but she died while he was out to sea. Wentworth, who came home a week earlier than Benwick, undertook to break the sad news to him stationed at Portsmouth. He 'wrote up for leave of absence, but without waiting the return, travelled night and day till he got to Portsmouth, rowed off to the Grappler that instant, and never left the poor fellow for a week'. Indeed, we sense an echo of Southey's eulogy on Nelson when Captain Harville exclaims: 'that's what he did, and nobody else could have saved poor James. You may think, Miss Elliot, whether he is dear to us!' (108). This episode is certainly not just a story of blighted love; together with the Dick Musgrove episode, it reveals an important aspect of Wentworth as an able leader.

The Royal Navy with numbers of able commanders and sailors full of esprit de corps under their command was admittedly the most regulated monolithic organization of the day, and, compared with it, the Army before Waterloo tended to be regarded as somewhat spineless and loose in discipline. Nelson himself remarked: 'Armies go so slow, that seamen think they never mean to get forward'.[26] But it happened that in a campaign on Corsica in 1794 Nelson conducted the siege of Bastia leading a joint force of his men and a body of soldiers, and reporting the unlooked-for spirited activity of the latter on the occasion, Southey observes: 'This is one proof, of many, that for our soldiers to equal our seamen, it is only necessary for them to be equally well commanded. . . . set their face toward a foe, and there is nothing within the reach of human achievement which they cannot perform'.[27] That the Army should follow the example of the Navy—this is what Southey intimates, and one could say that what Jane Austen tried to convey through *Persuasion* was a similar message—not, of course, to army soldiers but to English communities in general, especially to their leaders, the gentry.

The influence the Napoleonic Wars had on the British economy was many-faceted; their impact was not evenly felt by the nation, and those who derived rather unfair advantage from them were the landowners. Owing to Napoleon's Continental System and Britain's counter blockade, importation of corn from Europe stopped and the price of wheat in England during the war rose to an unusual level. Edwin Cannan reports that the average price of wheat in the 1790s was 55 shillings per quarter; but it rose to 82 shillings in the next ten years and to 106 shillings in 1810–13.[28]

This steep rise in wheat prices caused the costs of food to increase, and the poor suffered greatly. But for the landholders the wartime economy was quite beneficial; they could monopolize domestic markets and, as grain prices rose, the amount of rent charged by the landowners likewise rose. Indeed, 'at no period had the landed gentry been wealthier or happier, or more engrossed in the life of their pleasant country houses'.[29] Thus the gentry were in a sense thriving at the expense of lower orders, and this self-centred attitude was to become even more manifest in the framing and passing of the notorious Corn Law. This law which restricted the grain import to protect the domestic product had been repeatedly revised, and the law then in effect (passed in 1804) imposed heavy tariffs on imported corn when the price of wheat was under 63 shillings per quarter.[30] During the period of high grain prices the landlords paid little attention to the law, but towards the end of the war matters changed. In 1813 there was a good wheat harvest, and the temporary peace in 1814 not only '[turned] all our rich Navy Officers ashore', as Mr Shepherd remarks (17), but also brought foreign corn into Britain again. In consequence of these circumstances the price of wheat fell down to 69 shillings per quarter in May, 1814, and many landowners feared that their finances would be crippled if the importation of cheap foreign corn continued. Receiving urgent pressure from them the government suggested a modification of the Corn Law, and after much discussion it was finally proposed that the grain import should be altogether prohibited as long as the price of wheat in England remained under 80 shillings per quarter. The proposal, which would hinder free trade and prolong the high food costs, was extremely unpopular with the public, and there occurred a riot in London in early March of 1815 when the House of Commons was debating the Corn Bill. In spite of such fierce opposition, however, Parliament which consisted mostly of landowners passed the bill on 23 March, 1815. The Corn Law thus forcibly instituted by the landed interest lasted till it was repealed in 1846, and it has been described as 'one of the most naked pieces of class legislation in English history'.[31]

Persuasion was begun on 8 August, 1815, four and a half months after the passing of the Corn Law, and it is 'the only Austen novel with an explicit year'.³² The action of the novel covers the period from 'the summer of 1814' (8) to the end of February, 1815; significantly, it was the very time in which the Corn Bill was in hot debate inside and outside Parliament. There is no mention to the law or to the heated controversy over it in the novel, but the character of Sir Walter Elliot was no doubt influenced by and built on the whole process of the legislation, which 'made clear to many that the landed gentry did not regard themselves as heading and defending communities, but as looking after their class interest'.³³ But with what purpose did Jane Austen portray such a character? To criticize the self-centred attitude of the gentry was obviously a part of the author's intention, but not the whole—she was as obviously concerned about the welfare of society at large. The gentry thus engrossed in their own self-interest, the traditional fabric of society which had thrived under their care was in serious danger of disruption. In this critical situation Jane Austen turned her eyes to another organization ever familiar to her, the Royal Navy. Apparently the world of the Navy looks so different in nature from that of general rural communities that few would have thought of drawing an analogy between the two worlds. But Jane Austen knew that the system of hierarchy which formed the foundation of the military organization was in principle the same as that which governed local English communities, and that proper leadership was an essential factor for either fabric to function efficiently. In a time when the traditional system of English society was in danger of breakdown, the Royal Navy afforded an archetypal example of a well-working organization.

Let us finally take another look at the two protagonists of the novel, Wentworth and Anne, and weigh their attitudes towards hierarchy. We have tried to call up Captain Wentworth on board a ship of war with brilliant leadership, but Wentworth on shore is a wounded man—mentally, of course—and his wound has significantly affected his outlook on society. Since he was dismissed eight years ago as 'a young man, who had nothing but himself to recommend him'—as 'a stranger without alliance or fortune' (26, 27), he has come to set social privileges such as birth and lineage at defiance. During the walk to Winthrop Mary Musgrove took an opportunity to make him share her disdain of the Hayters, but her snobbish adherence to birth only incites 'a contemptuous glance ... which Anne perfectly knew the meaning of' (86). In the same episode there is also a scene which underlines his anti-establishmentarian attitude. In a hedgerow he walks with Louisa Musgrove; their conversation turns on the subject of 'interference' and, unaware of being overheard by Anne, he deprecates easy compliance and emphatically advocates the 'fortitude and strength of mind' (88). His words are permeated with his grudge against Anne, but they carry another significant connotation. As Kenneth L. Moler demonstrates, the romantic-revolutionary school of this period strongly 'opposed unreasonable submission to any of society's traditions and beliefs', and there is a decided echo of this kind of argument in his harangue to Louisa.[34]

With such a personal philosophy Wentworth has been often described as radical or even revolutionary; as several critics point out, however, his 'revolutionary' philosophy is by no means consistent. He requires 'strength' and 'firmness' from a woman, but his argument with his sister Mrs Croft reveals that 'he does not wish his putative wife's firmness of mind to extend to insisting on coming to sea with him'.[35] Moreover, while reviling 'idle interference' and stressing the necessity of 'resolution' to resist it (88), he apparently does not mind exercising his influence upon others. His impassioned speech to Louisa is a sort of brainwashing, and he is by no means unwilling to tolerate a 'yielding' character when it suits him.[36] But perhaps the most self-contradictory element in his philosophy is that he, who has lived in a world of strict hierarchy and must know the importance of rank and position, does not seem to pay any regard to those in the society on shore. As he himself later admits, Wentworth's mind is in a marked degree biased by his anger—anger against Anne and against 'the Elliot pride', which makes him behave like a mutinous sailor and blind to the analogy between the hierarchy in the Navy and that in the civil society. But the incidents at Lyme at last open his eyes; learning 'to distinguish between the steadiness of principle and the obstinacy of self-will, between the darings of heedlessness and the resolution of a collected mind' (242), he shakes off the arbitrarily mutinous attitude. Furthermore, at the end of the book we perceive a sign of his willing conformity to the system of the civilian organization, and that is his acceptance of Lady Russell.

Lady Russell plays an important role in the novel; she is a sort of touchstone, and the characters' mental attitude towards society is revealed by their attitude towards her. This could be best exemplified by the case of Anne. Anne's feelings towards Lady Russell—or rather, her feelings about the counsel which that lady gave to her eight years ago—are deeply ambiguous. By accepting her counsel—by allowing herself to be persuaded by her, Anne has become extremely unhappy. She has early lost her bloom, becoming so 'haggard' (6) and '[s]o altered that he [Wentworth] should not have known her again' (61). She feels that 'were any young person, in similar circumstances, to apply to her for counsel, they would never receive any of such certain immediate wretchedness, such uncertain future good' (29). She even intimates to us that the counsel was coloured by ambition. In her conversation with Charles Musgrove about his sisters' marriages, Anne remarks: 'What a blessing to young people to be in such hands! Your father and mother seem so totally free from all those ambitious feelings which have led to so much misconduct and misery, both in young and old!' (218). The 'ambitious feelings' here are obviously a distant allusion to those of Lady Russell, who 'had a value for rank and consequence' (11). Anne goes so far as to hint that her counsel was a piece of 'misconduct'. For all that, she 'did not blame Lady Russell, she did not blame herself for having been guided by her' (29). This sentiment of Anne is somewhat difficult to follow. Why does she not blame Lady Russell? On the day of their reunion Anne says to Wentworth that when she 'yielded' to Lady Russell's persuasion, she 'thought it was to duty' (244). Later, after 'trying impartially to judge of the right and wrong' with regard to herself, she declares that she was 'perfectly right' in submitting to Lady Russell. 'To me, she was in the place of a parent', she explains, 'and . . . if I had done otherwise . . . I should have suffered in my conscience' (246). In this context, the 'duty' she refers to seems to indicate the 'filial duty', but the word has wider and more serious connotations.

With Anne's explanation Wentworth does not seem to be 'perfectly' satisfied at once. But if Anne had compared the rejection in this case to a refusal of a young sailor to obey a command from his captain, Wentworth might have been satisfied on the spot. The refusal in the latter case would be a mutiny—a grave offence that would shake the foundations of the Navy as an organization—and Anne's rejection of Lady Russell's counsel would have had an equal significance. According to Harold Perkin, the eighteenth-century English society 'was firmly based on the twin principles of property and patronage',[37] and Lady Russell who has 'prejudices on the side of ancestry', yet is 'a benevolent, charitable, good woman' (11), could be regarded as an embodiment of the values and system of this society. When Anne says that she yielded to duty, therefore, this 'duty' not only means a duty to a surrogate parent but also implies a duty to the social organization. Anne's submission to Lady Russell's persuasion is indeed a token of her firm commitment to her society, and this position of hers never changes throughout the book. Her dissatisfaction with her irresponsible father and elder sister, her patient practice of charity, and her 'kind, compassionate visits' to Mrs Smith in her reduced circumstances (158)—all these arise from her strong sense of duty to society. In this respect Anne has a close affinity with Elinor Dashwood in *Sense and Sensibility* and Fanny Price in *Mansfield Park*; both characters also undergo severe hardships in performing what they believe to be right, and through their hardships both make a material contribution to the preservation of order. And yet Anne is not just a patient and passive preserver of order. That she could be an able commander is suggested in the scene of Louisa's accident at Lyme, where she keeps her presence of mind and gives proper directions to those around her. Indeed, Jane Austen by no means demanded the sacrifice of self to society. Well aware of the inevitability of hierarchy in human society, she rather wished that system to work for individuals, and indispensable to such a society was the presence of competent leaders—leaders who, as Frances Austen puts it, could make 'every class of persons pleased with their situation and eager to exert themselves in forwarding the public service'.

The picture presented at the end of the book is fairly auspicious. That

Wentworth 'was very well disposed to attach himself' to Lady Russell and 'could now value' her 'from his heart' (251) is a sure sign of his active participation in the reconstruction of the hierarchical system of the civil society. Indeed, the 'domestic virtues' of the naval profession referred to in the last sentence seem to imply its beneficial influence upon the society on shore. On the other hand, Sir Walter Elliot remains 'a foolish, spendthrift baronet' (248), showing no inclination to become a responsible landlord. Jane Austen no doubt wished for the self-reformation of the gentry; yet, given the bare-faced selfishness manifested in the enactment of the Corn Law, she perhaps did not entertain much hope for that. Actually, with rapid changes in social conditions after Waterloo, the old English society where 'the landowner was both competent and disinterested enough to be entrusted with responsibility for the general welfare' was never to revive.[38] Whatever course the English society followed in subsequent years, however, the value of the Royal Navy of the time as a model organization has not diminished, nor has the insight of Jane Austen who perceived an analogy between two different worlds lost its lustre. Indeed, there is no need to see in the novel any apostasy on the part of the author, who was consistently a sharp-sighted analyzer of the mechanism of society.

Notes

INTRODUCTION

1. G. M. Trevelyan, *History of England*, Illustrated edition (1926; rpt. London: Longman, 1973), p. 688.
2. Alistair M. Duckworth, *The Improvement of the Estate: A Study of Jane Austen's Novels* (Baltimore: Johns Hopkins Press, 1971).
3. Marilyn Butler, *Jane Austen and the War of Ideas* (Oxford: Clarendon Press, 1975).
4. Claudia L. Johnson, *Jane Austen: Women, Politics, and the Novel* (Chicago: University of Chicago Press, 1988).
5. Harold Perkin, *The Origins of Modern English Society 1780–1880* (London: Routledge & Kegan Paul, 1969), p. 17.
6. G. E. Mingay, *The Gentry: The Rise and Fall of a Ruling Class* (London: Longman, 1976), p. 164.

CHAPTER 1: General Tilney and Tyranny: *Northanger Abbey*

1. Duckworth, *The Improvement of the Estate*, p. 99.
2. B. C. Southam, '"Regulated Hatred" Revisited', in *Jane Austen: 'Northanger Abbey' and 'Persuasion': A Casebook*, ed. B.C. Southam (London: Macmillan, 1976), p. 125.
3. Ronald Paulson, *Representations of Revolution (1789–1820)* (New

Haven: Yale University Press, 1983), pp. 220–21.
4. Paulson, *Representations of Revolution*, p. 221.
5. Ann Radcliffe, *The Mysteries of Udolpho*, ed. Bonamy Dobrée (London: Oxford University Press, 1966), pp. 21, 329, 435.
6. Paulson, *Representations of Revolution*, p. 225.
7. Edmund Burke, *Reflections on the Revolution in France*, ed. Conor Cruise O'Brien (Harmondsworth: Penguin Books, 1968), p. 105.
8. Ann Radcliffe, *The Romance of the Forest*, ed. Chloe Chard (Oxford: Oxford University Press, 1986), p. 222.
9. Eleanor Sleath, *The Orphan of the Rhine*, ed. Devendra P. Varma (London: Polio Press, 1968), pp. 253–54.
10. Ann Radcliffe, *The Italian*, ed. Frederick Garber (London: Oxford University Press, 1968), pp. 166–78.
11. *The Italian*, p. 198.
12. For details of the government's repressive measures, see Warren Roberts, *Jane Austen and the French Revolution* (London: Macmillan, 1979), pp. 22–23.
13. Eugene Charlton Black, *The Association: British Extraparliamentary Political Organization 1769–1793* (Cambridge: Harvard University Press, 1963), pp. 237, 239.
14. E. P. Thompson, *The Making of the English Working Class* (Harmondsworth: Penguin Books, 1980), pp. 529–30.
15. *The Collected Works of Samuel Taylor Coleridge* 4, *The Friend* I, ed. Barbara E. Rooke (London: Routledge & Kegan Paul, 1969), pp. 218–19. This essay originally appeared in *The Friend*, no. 10 (19 October 1809).
16. In a humorous vein Coleridge describes how they were tracked by a spy who was sent down from the government to keep them under surveillance. See *The Collected Works of Samuel Taylor Coleridge* 7, *Biographia Literaria* I, ed. James Engell and W. Jackson Bate (Princeton: Princeton University Press, 1983), pp. 193–95.
17. Southam, '"Regulated Hatred" Revisited', pp. 123–24; Roberts, *Jane Austen and the French Revolution*, pp. 27–31.
18. Robert Hopkins, 'General Tilney and Affairs of State: The Political Gothic of *Northanger Abbey*', *Philological Quarterly* 57 (1978), 213–24.

19. Hopkins, 'General Tilney and Affairs of State', 218.
20. Hopkins, 'General Tilney and Affairs of State', 220.
21. *The Friend* I, p. 218.
22. B. C. Southam, 'General Tilney's Hot-houses: Some Recent Jane Austen Studies and Texts', *Ariel* 2 (1971), 55–56 and 59–61. See also his '*Sanditon*: The Seventh Novel' in *Jane Austen's Achievement*, ed. Juliet McMaster (London: Macmillan, 1976), pp. 1–26; in this article Southam himself makes an attempt at a historical interpretation of this matter.
23. David Spring, 'Interpreters of Jane Austen's Social World: Literary Critics and Historians', in *Jane Austen: New Perspectives*, ed. Janet Todd (New York: Holmes & Meier, 1983), pp. 53–72.
24. Spring, 'Interpreters of Jane Austen's Social World', p. 64.
25. Spring, 'Interpreters of Jane Austen's Social World', p. 65.
26. Southam, in '*Sanditon*: The Seventh Novel', sees in the General's 'pious concern for the welfare of his servants' a mocking allusion to Count Rumford, the inventor of the Rumford fireplace, who 'prided himself as a philanthropist-thinker' (p. 14).
27. Tony Tanner, *Jane Austen* (London: Macmillan, 1986), p. 65.
28. Edward Copeland, *Women Writing about Money: Women's Fiction in England, 1790–1820* (Cambridge: Cambridge University Press, 1995), pp. 92–93.
29. Tanner, *Jane Austen*, p. 65.
30. Christopher Kent, '"Real Solemn History" and Social History', in *Jane Austen in a Social Context*, ed. David Monaghan (London: Macmillan, 1981), pp. 98–99.
31. Minako Enomoto, 'Ōsuten ni okeru shōsetsu-bengo no haikei' [The Background of Jane Austen's Vindication of the Novel] in her *Ōsuten no shōsetsu to sono shūhen* [The Novels of Jane Austen and Their Backgrounds] (Tokyo: Eihōsha, 1984), pp. 202–34.
32. Jane Aiken Hodge, *The Double Life of Jane Austen* (London: Hodder and Stoughton, 1972), pp. 177–78. Quoting the novel-defence passage, Hodge remarks: 'This is no unpublished novelist speaking' (p. 178).

33. Howard S. Babb, *Jane Austen's Novels: The Fabric of Dialogue* (Columbus: Ohio State University Press, 1962), p. 109.

CHAPTER 2: Marianne and Mary: *Sense and Sensibility*

1. Molière, *The Misanthrope and Other Plays*, trans. by John Wood (Harmondsworth: Penguin Books, 1959), p. 27.
2. Molière, *The Misanthrope*, p. 26.
3. Erich Auerbach, *Mimesis: The Representation of Reality in Western Literature*, trans. by Willard R. Trask (Princeton: Princeton University Press, 1968), p. 365.
4. Tanner, *Jane Austen*, p. 85.
5. For a discussion of Elinor's screening, see Tanner, *Jane Austen*, pp. 85–86.
6. For my discussion of the destructive power of feelings and the rules of propriety as its restraint, I owe much to Jane Nardin, *Those Elegant Decorums: The Concept of Propriety in Jane Austen's Novels* (Albany: State University of New York Press, 1973), pp. 41–43.
7. Duckworth, *The Improvement of Estate*, p. 107.
8. Babb, *The Fabric of Dialogue*, pp. 65–69; the quoted phrase is found in pp. 66–67.
9. Auerbach, *Mimesis*, p. 370.
10. Auerbach, *Mimesis*, p. 370.
11. Claudia Johnson, *Jane Austen: Women, Politics, and the Novel*, pp. 49–72.
12. LeRoy W. Smith, *Jane Austen and the Drama of Woman* (London: Macmillan, 1983), pp. 69–86.
13. Mary Poovey, *The Proper Lady and the Woman Writer: Ideology as Style in the Works of Mary Wollstonecraft, Mary Shelley, and Jane Austen* (Chicago: University of Chicago Press, 1984), pp. 183–94.
14. Johnson, *Jane Austen*, p. 61.
15. Mary Wollstonecraft, *A Short Residence in Sweden, Norway and Denmark*, and William Godwin, *Memoirs of the Author of The Rights of*

Woman, ed. Richard Holmes (Harmondsworth: Penguin Books, 1987), pp. 256–57; hereafter cited either as *A Short Residence* or *Memoirs*.
16. Wollstonecraft, *A Short Residence*, p. 73.
17. Godwin, *Memoirs*, p. 237.
18. Claire Tomalin, *The Life and Death of Mary Wollstonecraft* (London: Weidenfeld and Nicolson, 1974), p. 146.
19. Godwin, *Memoirs*, p. 242.
20. See Chapman, 'Introductory Note to *Sense and Sensibility*', *Novels of Jane Austen*, vol. I, p. xiii. Wollstonecraft died on 10 September, 1797.
21. Tomalin, *Mary Wollstonecraft*, p. 110.
22. Tomalin notes thus: 'Sir William East, a neighbour of the Mrs Cotton with whom Mary stayed in Berkshire in 1796 after her second suicide attempt, is said to have shown her much kindness. The son of Sir William East was a resident pupil in the house of Jane Austen's father' (*Mary Wollstonecraft*, p. 302).
23. R. W. Chapman, *Jane Austen: Facts and Problems* (Oxford: Clarendon Press, 1948), pp. 121–29; see also his 'Jane Austen's Methods', *Times Literary Supplement*, 9 February, 1922, 81–82.
24. *Jane Austen's Letters*, p. 275.

CHAPTER 3: Too Much Antipathy towards Too Much Formality: *Pride and Prejudice*

1. *Jane Austen's Letters*, p. 201.
2. Elizabeth's laughter has constantly drawn critical attention, and has often been discussed in terms of the role or meaning of laughter in the novel; see, for example, Duckworth, *The Improvement of the Estate*, pp. 132–40; Patricia Meyer Spacks, 'Austen's Laughter', *Women's Studies* 15 (1988), 72–76; Audrey Bilger, *Laughing Feminism: Subversive Comedy in Frances Burney, Maria Edgeworth, and Jane Austen* (Detroit: Wayne State University Press, 1998), pp. 71–75; Elvira Casal, 'Laughing at Mr. Darcy: Wit and Sexuality in *Pride and Prejudice*', *Persuasions: The Jane Austen Journal On-Line* 22.1 (2001).

3. David M. Shapard ed., *The Annotated Pride and Prejudice* (2004; rpt. New York: Anchor Books, 2007), p. 573.
4. According to *The Book of the Ranks and Dignities of British Society*, attributed to Charles Lamb (1805; rpt. London: Jonathan Cape, 1924, p. 135), a wife of a knight takes precedence over a daughter of a baronet, and so Elizabeth stands second to Lady Russell among the women in the neighbourhood. Within the family she as an eldest daughter of course takes the leading position.
5. For a discussion of the rigid formality in the novel's world, see Tanner, *Jane Austen*, pp. 130–41. As regards the rules of propriety in this novel, see also Jane Nardin's examination in *Those Elegant Decorums*, pp. 47–61.
6. For the details of the reform movements in this period, see Maurice J. Quinlan, *Victorian Prelude: A History of English Manners 1700–1830* (1941; rpt. Hamden, Connecticut: Archon Books, 1965); Ford K. Brown, *Fathers of the Victorians: The Age of Wilberforce* (Cambridge: Cambridge University Press, 1961); Edward J. Bristow, *Vice and Vigilance: Purity Movements in Britain since 1700* (Dublin: Gill and Macmillan, 1977).
7. In his *Disciplining Love: Austen and the Modern Man* (Columbus: Ohio State University Press, 2007), Michael Kramp propounds a very different and far more favourable view on Darcy's relationship with Bingley. He argues that '*Pride and Prejudice* dramatizes how England and its ancestral leaders are beginning to recognize the social potential of new classes of men', and 'Darcy's concern for and tutelage of Bingley . . . suggest the hero's recognition that wealthy men of trade like Bingley are becoming vital resources in England's future—and these men must be taught to discipline their passions to ensure their maturation as stable men of the nation' (pp. 76, 80).
8. See 'Chronology of *Pride and Prejudice*', in *The Novels of Jane Austen*, vol. II, pp. 400–08. Chapman's view is thoroughly re-examined by Shapard in *The Annotated Pride and Prejudice*, pp. 713–23. He demonstrates that the flaws found in Chapman's theory concerning the use of the 1811–12 calendar are by no means trivial and thus warns

us against an implicit faith in this theory. At the same time, he also dismisses 'the possibility that she [Jane Austen] could have envisaged another specific pair of years besides 1811–12' (p. 722).

9. *The Novels of Jane Austen*, vol. V, p. 12. In his 'Introduction' to his edition of *Pride and Prejudice* in *The Cambridge Edition of Works of Jane Austen* (Cambridge: Cambridge University Press, 2006), Pat Rogers with persuasive eloquence advocates the theory that the action of the novel belongs to the 1790s rather than to 1810s (pp. liii–lxii). In 'Chronology of *Pride and Prejudice*' Chapman, though he admits the possibility of this, nonetheless remarks: 'I feel a certain difficulty in supposing that, in publishing *Pride and Prejudice* in 1813, Miss Austen definitely conceived its action as taking place some ten years (or more) earlier' (*The Novels of Jane Austen*, vol. II, p. 407). In view of Jane Austen's scrupulousness shown in the 'Advertisement' to *Northanger Abbey*, Chapman's judgement seems to have significant weight that cannot be ignored.
10. See, for example, Maaja A. Stewart, *Domestic Realities and Imperial Fictions: Jane Austen's Novels in Eighteenth-Century Contexts* (Athens: University of Georgia Press, 1993), pp. 59–71. Stewart discusses the relationship between *Pride and Prejudice* and the earlier comedy of manners in terms of the opposition between wit and judgement.
11. Henry Fielding, *Joseph Andrews*, ed. Martin C. Battestin (Middletown, Connecticut: Wesleyan University Press, 1967), p. 9.
12. Henry Fielding, *The Covent-Garden Journal and A Plan of the Universal Register-Office*, ed. Bertrand A. Goldgar (Oxford: Clarendon Press, 1988), p. 300. The reference to Horace is to *Epistles*, I. vi,15–16; Abbé Bellegarde is Jean Baptiste Morvan de Bellegarde (1648–1734), whose *Reflexions sur le ridicule, et sur les moyens de l'eviter* was published in 1697. As these references show, Fielding's argument about the ridiculous, including that in the Preface to *Joseph Audrews*, was by no means original to him.
13. Hannah More, *Strictures on the Modern System of Female Education* (London: T. Cadell Jun. and W. Davies, 1799), I, pp. 12, 16.
14. Robert Hole, 'Introduction', in his edition of *Selected Writings of*

Hannah More (London: William Pickering, 1996), p. xxviii.
15. Samuel Kliger, 'Jane Austen's *Pride and Prejudice* in the Eighteenth-Century Mode', *University of Toronto Quarterly* 16 (1947), 357–70; rpt. *Jane Austen: Critical Assessments*, ed. Ian Littlewood (The Banks, East Sussex: Helm Information, 1998), vol. III, pp. 254–68; the quotation is found in p. 255.
16. Kenneth L. Moler, *Pride and Prejudice: A Study in Artistic Economy* (Boston: Twayne, 1989), p. 49.
17. A. Walton Litz, *Jane Austen: A Study of Her Artistic Development* (London: Chatto & Windus, 1965), pp. 104–05. Another representative of this school that regard Elizabeth as standing for one pole of the antithesis is Alistair M. Duckworth, (*The Improvement of the Estate*, pp. 116–43). As is hinted in the text, those critics who hold Elizabeth's attitude to be 'radical' or 'subversive' are also included in this group. On the other hand, the only critic that points out Elizabeth's balanced view is Jane Nardin (160).
18. *The Letters of Mary Russell Mitford*, ed. R. Brimley Johnson (London: John Lane The Bodley Head, 1925), p. 121. The letter is to Sir William Elford, dated December 20, 1814.
19. *Letters of Mary Russell Mitford*, pp. 121–22.
20. See, for example, Duckworth, *The Improvement of the Estate*, p. 120; Nardin, *Those Elegant Decorums*, p. 58–59.
21. Nardin in *Those Elegant Decorums* discusses this shift in Elizabeth's view of the rules of behaviour in terms of moral rules and fashionable rules (pp. 59–60).
22. G. E. Mingay, *English Landed Society in the Eighteenth Century* (London: Routledge and Kegan Paul, 1963), p. 14.
23. Muriel Jaeger, *Before Victoria: Changing Standards and Behaviour 1787–1837* (London: Chatto & Windus, 1956), p. 129. All further references to the book are to this edition and are included in the text.

CHAPTER 4: The Other Side of an Orderly World: *Mansfield Park*

1. Cf. the relevant passages in Chapter 3.
2. For my discussion of the Sotherton episode I owe much to Ann Banfield, 'The Moral Landscape of *Mansfield Park*', *Nineteenth-Century Fiction* 26 (1971), 5–11; Tony Tanner, *Jane Austen*, pp. 159–62.
3. 'as the starling said' is a reference to a passage from Laurence Sterne's *Sentimental Journey* (1768) in the chapter entitled 'The Passport, The Hotel at Paris'.
4. R. A. Cox, *Mansfield Park* (Notes on English Literature) (Oxford: Basil Blackwell, 1970), p. 74.
5. Nardin, *Those Elegant Decorums*, p. 104.
6. David Lodge, 'The Vocabulary of *Mansfield Park*', in his *Language of Fiction: Essays in Criticism and Verbal Analysis of the English Novel* (London: Routledge and Kegan Paul, 1966), pp. 110–11.
7. Jaeger, *Before Victoria*, p. 73.
8. *Diary and Letters of Madame d'Arblay*, ed. Charlotte Barrett, 4 vols. (1893), II, p. 519, as quoted in Joyce Hemlow, 'Fanny Burney and the Courtesy Books', *PMLA* 65 (1950), 748.
9. She writes thus: 'You have by no means raised my curiosity after Caleb [Hannah More's *Cœlebs in Search of a Wife*];—My disinclination for it before was affected, but now it is real; I do not like the Evangelicals' (*Jane Austen's Letters*, pp. 169–70). Later in her letter to Fanny Knight (written on 18 November, 1814) she again refers to Evangelicals: 'And as to there being any objection from his *Goodness*, from the danger of his becoming even Evangelical, I cannot admit *that*. I am by no means convinced that we ought not all to be Evangelicals, & am at least persuaded that they who are so from Reason & Feeling, must be happiest & safest' (*Jane Austen's Letters*, p. 280). This time her tone is apparently favourable to Evangelicals, so that the passage is sometimes regarded as indicative of her change of view. But this is not necessarily so; her antipathy towards the Evangelical cause can be still perceived underlying the passage.
10. Sybil Rosenfeld, 'Jane Austen and Private Theatricals', *Essays and*

Studies 15 (1962), 42–43.

11. For an account of the relationship between the gentry and the common people during the eighteenth century, see Robert W. Malcolmson, *Popular Recreations in English Society 1700–1850* (Cambridge: Cambridge University. Press, 1973), especially chap. 4 and 8.
12. B. C. Southam, '*Sanditon*: The Seventh Novel', pp. 4–5.

CHAPTER 5: Self-Deception and Superiority Complex: *Emma*

1. Johnson, *Jane Austen*, p. 130.
2. Duckworth, *The Improvement of the Estate*, p. 174. For a 'deciphering' of the Sotherton episode, see Tanner, *Jane Austen*, pp. 159–62.
3. The term is used by Harold Perkin in *The Origins of Modern English Society*; the following quotations in this paragraph are from Chap. 2, 'The Old Society', p. 24. Cf. Roy Porter, *English Society in the Eighteenth Century* (Harmondsworth: Penguin Books, 1982), Chap. 2, 'The Social Order'.
4. The only person who could be called a malcontent is Jane Fairfax, who at one point deplores her lot by drawing an analogy between a governess and a slave (300–01). But even this hardly amounts to criticism of the hierarchical system; she is discontented not so much with society as with Frank Churchill (as for governesses, though, Jane Austen no doubt sympathized with Jane Fairfax's view of their 'slavish' condition).
5. Oliver MacDonagh, *Jane Austen: Real and Imagined Worlds* (New Haven: Yale University Press, 1991), pp. 134–35.
6. Nardin, *Those Elegant Decorums*, p. 112; in my discussion of Emma's character and her way of estimating others, I am indebted to Nardin's analyses.
7. Nardin, *Those Elegant Decorums*, p. 113.
8. G.E. Mingay, *The Gentry*, p. 163.
9. In analysing the passage describing Emma's visit to the poor family, Jane Nardin argues: 'Obviously we are seeing Emma, the giver of

charity, through Emma's own eyes—and not through Jane Austen's. Just as Harriet Smith ... provided Emma with an opportunity to display her own power and wisdom ... so now the poor family serves a similar function in ministering to Emma's sense of superiority. In view of the fact that Emma's attempts to direct Harriet's destiny turn out so badly, the reader is surely meant to suspect that she does not understand the poor family and its needs as well as she herself thinks'. 'Charity in *Emma*', *Studies in the Novel* 7(1975), 62.
10. Henry Fielding, *Amelia*, ed. Martin C. Battestin (Middletown: Wesleyan University Press, 1984), p. 90. This seems to have been Fielding's pet idea; as Battestin points out in the note, he proposes the same view in 'An Essay on the Knowledge of the Characters of Men' (1743).
11. Claire Tomalin, *Jane Austen: A Life* (New York: Alfred A. Knopf, 1997), p. 85.
12. Spring, 'Interpreters of Jane Austen's Social World', p. 61; Spring borrowed the term 'pseudo-gentry' from Alan Everitt. In her biography, *Jane Austen: A Literary Life* (London: Macmillan, 1991), Jan Fergus criticizes the term, remarking that it 'carries too many connotations of fraudulence to be accurate' (p. 47).
13. Nardin, 'Charity in *Emma*', 67.
14. Beth Fowkes Tobin, 'The Moral and Political Economy of Property in Austen's *Emma*', in her *Superintending the Poor: Charitable Ladies and Paternal Landlords in British Fiction, 1770–1860* (New Haven: Yale University Press, 1993), p. 69.
15. Duckworth, *The Improvement of the Estate*, p. 158; for a discussion about Mrs Elton's role as a caricature of Emma, see also Nardin, 'Charity in *Emma*', 64–65.
16. Mark Parker, 'The End of Emma: Drawing the Boundaries of Class in Austen', *Journal of English and Germanic Philology* 91 (1992), 347.

CHAPTER 6: An Organization that Works: *Persuasion*

1. Nina Auerbach, 'O Brave New World: Evolution and Revolution in

Persuasion', *ELH*, 39 (1972); rpt. *Jane Austen: Critical Assessments*, vol. IV, p. 482.

2. Tanner, *Jane Austen*, pp. 229, 249. For early criticism that speaks of the 'decline', see, for example, Joseph M. Duffy, Jr, 'Structure and Idea in Jane Austen's *Persuasion*', *Nineteenth-Century Fiction*, 8 (1953–54); rpt. *Jane Austen: Critical Assessments*, vol. IV, p. 398. For a discussion of the shift in Jane Austen's attitude in terms of social change, see Duckworth, *The Improvement of the Estate*, pp. 179–208; Julia Prewitt Brown, *Jane Austen's Novels: Social Change and Literary Form* (Cambridge, Massachusetts: Harvard University Press, 1979), pp. 127–50; David Monaghan, *Jane Austen: Structure and Social Vision* (London: Macmillan, 1980), pp. 143–62.
3. Spring, 'Interpreters of Jane Austen's Social World', p. 65.
4. Mingay, *The Gentry*, p. 164.
5. We are told in Vol. II Ch. II that Anne could not 'return from any stroll of solitary indulgence in her father's grounds, or *any visit of charity in the village*, without wondering whether she might see him [Captain Benwick] or hear of him' (133; emphasis added).
6. Monaghan, *Structure and Social Vision*, p. 3. The 'ritual means' here refers to behaviour in formal social occasions ('social rituals') such as 'balls, dinners, evening-parties and visits' (p.1). The citation from Burke is from *First Letter on a Regicide Peace* (1796).
7. Keiko Parker, '"What Part of Bath Do You Think They Will Settle In?": Jane Austen's Use of Bath in *Persuasion*', *Persuasions* 23 (2001), 166–76.
8. Parker, 'Jane Austen's Use of Bath', 169. Maggie Lane, in her *A Charming Place: Bath in the Life and Times of Jane Austen* (Bath: Millstream Books, 1988), pointing out that in the early years of the nineteenth century the building project in Camden-place (now Camden Crescent) was not completed and the ground was 'shaky', remarks that 'the choice of Camden Crescent, with its subtle yet glorious symbolism, for Sir Walter Elliot, is surely unsurpassed' (pp. 38, 40).
9. Parker, 'Jane Austen's Use of Bath', 175.

10. Roger Sales, *Jane Austen and Representations of Regency England* (London: Routledge, 1994), p. 179.
11. Janet Todd and Antje Blank, 'Explanatory Notes', in their edition of *Persuasion* (Cambridge: Cambridge University Press, 2006), p. 369.
12. Michael Lewis, *A Social History of the Navy 1793–1815* (London: George Allen & Unwin, 1960), p. 31.
13. Lewis, *A Social History of the Navy*, p. 34. As he points out, there is one disadvantage in both Marshall's and O'Byrne's works, and that is that they include only such men as were living at the time of their compilation (Marshall in 1823, and O'Byrne in 1845), and thus omit all the officers who died before those dates. In respect of the officers' parentage there is another inadequacy. Among the contributors to their works, many were reticent on the question of 'Father's name?'. In Lewis's table the officers whose parents were 'business and commercial men' account for only 3.9 %, but he concludes that, 'had every officer of "business and commerce" affinities come out boldly with the information, that category would have been the largest of all' (p. 30).
14. For a detail of 'the naval hierarchy' and 'the ship hierarchy', see Lewis, *A Social History of the Navy*, pp. 181–201 and pp. 228–87.
15. Brian Lavery, *Nelson's Navy: The Ships, Men and Organisation 1793–1815* (London: Conway Maritime Press, 1990), p. 112.
16. Lavery, *Nelson's Navy*, p. 194.
17. J. H. and Edith C. Hubback, *Jane Austen's Sailor Brothers* (1906; rpt. Stroud, Gloucestershire: Ian Hodgkins, 1986), p. 77.
18. Brian Southam, *Jane Austen and the Navy*, 2nd ed. (London: National Maritime Museum, 2005).
19. In *Jane Austen and the Navy* Southam notes: 'Until 1811, the record of a ship's punishments could only be derived from the Captain's or the Master's log; and as these were inspected when a voyage or tour of duty was completed, any excesses would come to light long after the event, far too late to restrain a tyrannical Captain. However, as the war progressed, humanitarian views began to gain ground. A marked change of attitude towards Service discipline became evident. In March 1811, the system of oversight was tightened, the Return of

Offences and Punishment now to be made on a quarterly basis. The record was submitted by ships' Captains to their immediate superiors and passed on, if appropriate, with Flag-Officers' comments, for scrutiny at the Admiralty' (pp. 288–89). Southam adds that in consequence of this 'tightened system of oversight', Francis ran foul of the Admiralty in 1813 for the frequency of punishments on board the *Elephant* (a ship he was then in command of)—a circumstance which Jane Austen probably did not know of.

20. Geoffrey Callender, ed., *Southey's Life of Nelson* (London: J. M. Dent, 1922), pp. 32 and 268.
21. *Jane Austen's Letters*, p. 235. Previous to Southey's *Life*, several biographies of Nelson already appeared, including James Stanier Clarke and John M'Arthur's *The Life of Admiral Lord Nelson* (1809). Clarke, who later became Prince Regent's librarian and advised Jane Austen to write a 'Romance', had served as a chaplain in ships of war in the 1790s.
22. Jocelyn Harris, *A Revolution Almost beyond Expression: Jane Austen's Persuasion* (Newark: University of Delaware Press, 2007), p. 91. Since Francis is not mentioned in Southey's *Life*, most critics, including Southam, are inclined to believe that she did not read it. According to Harris, however, the very fact that he is not mentioned suggests that she did read it (p. 98).
23. *Life of Nelson*, p. 106.
24. *Jane Austen's Sailor Brothers*, p. 156.
25. *Life of Nelson*, pp. 267–68.
26. *Life of Nelson*, p. 62.
27. *Life of Nelson*, p. 63.
28. Edwin Cannan, *A History of the Theories of Production and Distribution in English Political Economy from 1776 to 1848*, 2nd ed. (London: P. S. King & Son, 1903), p. 149.
29. G. M. Trevelyan, *English Social History: A Survey of Six Centuries, Chaucer to Queen Victoria*, 3rd ed. (London: Longman, 1946), p. 466.
30. For a detail of the Corn Laws, see Donald Grove Barnes, *A History of the English Corn Laws from 1660 to 1846* (New York: F. S. Crofts,

1930), especially Chapter VII, where he closely follows the whole process of the enactment of the Corn Law of 1815.
31. Robert Blake, *The Conservative Party from Peel to Churchill* (1970; rpt. London: Fontana, 1972), p. 15.
32. Jo Modert, 'Chronology within the Novels', J. David Grey, ed., *The Jane Austen Handbook* (London: Athlone Press, 1986), p. 58. For a detailed discussion on the chronology in *Persuasion*, see Ellen Moody, 'A Calendar for *Persuasion*' (http://www.jimandellen.org/austen/persuasion.calendar.html).
33. Janet Todd and Antje Blank, 'Introduction', in their edition of *Persuasion*, p. xxxii.
34. Kenneth L. Moler, *Jane Austen's Art of Allusion* (1968; rpt. Lincoln: University of Nebraska Press, 1977), pp. 187–223; the quotation is from p. 196.
35. Mary Waldron, *Jane Austen and the Fiction of Her Time* (Cambridge: Cambridge University Press, 1999), p. 141.
36. Claudia Johnson, pointing out that 'Louisa's strength of mind is really only persuadability to him in disguise', observes thus: 'Wentworth disdains the feeble malleability of "too yielding and indecisive a character" when it defies him as Anne's did, but he does not seem to mind or even to notice the same qualities when they malleably conform to his own influence' (*Jane Austen: Women, Politics, and the Novel*, p. 156).
37. Perkin, *Origins of Modern English Society*, p. 38.
38. Perkin, *Origins of Modern English Society*, p. 28.

Bibliography

I. Works by Jane Austen

The Novels of Jane Austen. Ed. R. W. Chapman. 5 vols. 3rd edition. London: Oxford University Press, 1932–34; reprinted with revisions 1965–69.
The Cambridge Edition of the Works of Jane Austen. 9 vols. Ed. Janet Todd et al. Cambridge: Cambridge University Press, 2005–08.
Jane Austen's Letters. Collected and edited by Deirdre Le Faye. 3rd edition. Oxford: Oxford University Press, 1995.

II. Works Cited in the Text

Anon. [Charles Lamb]. *The Book of the Ranks and Dignities of British Society.* 1805; rpt. London: Jonathan Cape, 1924.
Auerbach, Erich. *Mimesis: The Representation of Reality in Western Literature.* Trans. by Willard R. Trask. Princeton: Princeton University Press, 1968.
Auerbach, Nina. 'O Brave New World: Evolution and Revolution in *Persuasion*'. *ELH*, 39 (1972); rpt. *Jane Austen: Critical Assessments.* Ed. Ian Littlewood. The Banks, East Sussex: Helm Information, 1998, vol. IV, pp. 482–96.
Babb, Howard S. *Jane Austen's Novels: The Fabric of Dialogue.* Columbus: Ohio State University Press, 1962.

Banfield, Ann. 'The Moral Landscape of *Mansfield Park*', *Nineteenth-Century Fiction* 26 (1971), 1–24.

Barnes, Donald Grove. *A History of the English Corn Laws from 1660 to 1846*. New York: F. S. Crofts, 1930.

Bilger, Audrey. *Laughing Feminism: Subversive Comedy in Frances Burney, Maria Edgeworth, and Jane Austen*. Detroit: Wayne State University Press, 1998.

Black, Eugene Charlton. *The Association: British Extraparliamentary Political Organization 1769–1793*. Cambridge: Harvard University Press, 1963.

Blake, Robert. *The Conservative Party from Peel to Churchill*. 1970; rpt. London: Fontana, 1972.

Bristow, Edward J. *Vice and Vigilance: Purity Movements in Britain since 1700*. Dublin: Gill and Macmillan, 1977.

Brown, Ford K. *Fathers of the Victorians: The Age of Wilberforce*. Cambridge: Cambridge University Press, 1961.

Brown, Julia Prewitt. *Jane Austen's Novels: Social Change and Literary Form*. Cambridge, Massachusetts: Harvard University Press, 1979.

Burke, Edmund. *Reflections on the Revolution in France*. Ed. Conor Cruise O'Brien. Harmondsworth: Penguin Books, 1968.

Butler, Marilyn. *Jane Austen and the War of Ideas*. Oxford: Clarendon Press, 1975.

Cannan, Edwin. *A History of the Theories of Production and Distribution in English Political Economy from 1776 to 1848*. 2nd ed. London: P. S. King & Son, 1903.

Casal, Elvira. 'Laughing at Mr. Darcy: Wit and Sexuality in *Pride and Prejudice*'. *Persuasions: The Jane Austen Journal On-Line* 22.1 (2001).

Chapman, R. W. *Jane Austen: Facts and Problems*. Oxford: Clarendon Press, 1948.

——. 'Jane Auste's Methods'. *Times Literary Supplement*, 9 February, 1922, 81–82.

Coleridge, Samuel Taylor. *Biographia Literaria. The Collected Works of Samuel Taylor Coleridge*, vol. 7. Ed. James Engell and W. Jackson Bate. Princeton: Princeton University Press, 1983.

——. *The Friend. The Collected Works of Samuel Taylor Coleridge*, vol. 4. Ed. Barbara E. Rooke. London: Routledge & Kegan Paul, 1969.

Copeland, Edward. *Women Writing about Money: Women's Fiction in England, 1790–1820.* Cambridge: Cambridge University Press, 1995.

Cox, R. A. *Mansfield Park* (Notes on English Literature). Oxford: Basil Blackwell, 1970.

Duckworth, Alistair M. *The Improvement of the Estate: A Study of Jane Austen's Novels.* Baltimore: Johns Hopkins Press.

Duffy, Jr., Joseph M. 'Structure and Idea in Jane Austen's *Persuasion*'. *Nineteenth-Century Fiction*, 8 (1953–54). Rpt. *Jane Austen: Critical Assessments*. Ed. Ian Littlewood. The Banks, East Sussex: Helm Information, 1998, vol. IV, pp. 396–409.

Enomoto, Minako. *Ōsuten no shōsetsu to sono shūhen* [The Novels of Jane Austen and Their Backgrounds]. Tokyo: Eihosha, 1984.

Fergus, Jan. *Jane Austen: A Literary Life.* London: Macmillan, 1991.

Fielding, Henry. *Amelia*. Ed. Martin C. Battestin. Middletown, Connecticut: Wesleyan University Press, 1984.

——. *The Covent-Garden Journal and A Plan of the Universal Register-Office*. Ed. Bertrand A. Goldgar. Oxford: Clarendon Press, 1988.

——. *Joseph Andrews*. Ed. Martin C. Battestin. Middletown, Connecticut: Wesleyan University Press, 1967.

Harris, Jocelyn. *A Revolution Almost beyond Expression: Jane Austen's* Persuasion. Newark: University of Delaware Press, 2007.

Hemlow, Joyce. 'Fanny Burney and the Courtesy Books'. *PMLA* 65 (1950), 732–61.

Hodge, Jane Aiken. *The Double Life of Jane Austen.* London: Hodder and Stoughton, 1972.

Hopkins, Robert. 'General Tilney and Affairs of State: The Political Gothic of *Northanger Abbey*'. *Philological Quarterly* 57 (1978), 213–24.

Hubback, J. H. and Edith C. *Jane Austen's Sailor Brothers*. 1906; rpt. Stroud, Gloucestershire: Ian Hodgkins, 1986.

Jaeger, Muriel. *Before Victoria: Changing Standards and Behaviour 1787–1837*. London: Chatto & Windus, 1956.

Johnson, Claudia L. *Jane Austen: Women, Politics, and the Novel.* Chicago:

University of Chicago Press, 1988.

Kent, Christopher. '"Real Solemn History" and Social History'. In *Jane Austen in a Social Context*. Ed. David Monaghan. London: Macmillan, 1981, pp. 86–104.

Kliger, Samuel. 'Jane Austen's *Pride and Prejudice* in the Eighteenth-Century Mode'. *University of Toronto Quarterly* 16 (1947). Rpt. *Jane Austen: Critical Assessments*. Ed. Ian Littlewood. The Banks, East Sussex: Helm Information, 1998, vol. III, pp. 254–68.

Kramp, Michael. *Disciplining Love: Austen and the Modern Man*. Columbus: Ohio State University Press, 2007.

Lane, Maggie. *A Charming Place: Bath in the Life and Times of Jane Austen*. Bath: Millstream Books, 1988.

Lavery, Brian. *Nelson's Navy: The Ships, Men and Organisation 1793–1815*. London: Conway Maritime Press, 1990.

Lewis, Michael. *A Social History of the Navy 1793–1815*. London: George Allen & Unwin, 1960.

Litz, A. Walton. *Jane Austen: A Study of Her Artistic Development*. London: Chatto & Windus, 1965.

Lodge, David. 'The Vocabulary of *Mansfield Park*'. In *Language of Fiction: Essays in Criticism and Verbal Analysis of the English Novel*. London: Routledge and Kegan Paul, 1966, pp. 94–113.

MacDonagh, Oliver. *Jane Austen: Real and Imagined Worlds*. New Haven: Yale University Press, 1991.

Malcolmson, Robert W. *Popular Recreations in English Society 1700–1850*. Cambridge: Cambridge University Press, 1973.

Mingay, G. E. *English Landed Society in the Eighteenth Century*. London: Routledge and Kegan Paul, 1963.

——. *The Gentry: The Rise and Fall of a Ruling Class*. London: Longman, 1976.

Mitford, Mary Russell. *The Letters of Mary Russell Mitford*. Ed. R. Brimley Johnson. London: John Lane The Bodley Head, 1925.

Modert, Jo. 'Chronology within the Novels'. *The Jane Austen Handbook*. Ed. J. David Grey. London: Athlone Press, 1986, pp. 53–59.

Moler, Kenneth L. *Jane Austen's Art of Allusion*. 1968; rpt. Lincoln: University of Nebraska Press, 1977.

———. *Pride and Prejudice: A Study in Artistic Economy.* Boston: Twayne, 1989.

Molière. *The Misanthrope and Other Plays.* Trans. by John Wood. Harmondsworth: Penguin Books, 1959.

Monaghan, David. *Jane Austen: Structure and Social Vision.* London: Macmillan, 1980.

Moody, Ellen. 'A Calendar for *Persuasion*'. http://www.jimandellen.org/austen/persuasion.calendar.html.

More, Hannah. *Strictures on the Modern System of Female Education.* 2vols. London: T. Cadell Jun. and W. Davies, 1799.

———. *Selected Writings of Hannah More.* Ed. Robert Hole. London: William Pickering, 1996.

Nardin, Jane. 'Charity in *Emma*', *Studies in the Novel* 7(1975), 61–72.

———. *Those Elegant Decorums: The Concept of Propriety in Jane Austen's Novels.* Albany: State University of New York Press, 1973.

Parker, Keiko. '"What Part of Bath Do You Think They Will Settle In?": Jane Austen's Use of Bath in *Persuasion*'. *Persuasions* 23 (2001), 166–76.

Parker, Mark. 'The End of Emma: Drawing the Boundaries of Class in Austen'. *Journal of English and Germanic Philology* 91 (1992), 344–59.

Paulson, Ronald. *Representations of Revolution (1789–1820).* New Haven: Yale University Press, 1883.

Perkin, Harold. *The Origins of Modern English Society 1780–1880.* London: Routledge & Kegan Paul, 1969.

Poovey, Mary. *The Proper Lady and the Woman Writer: Ideology as Style in the Works of Mary Wollstonecraft, Mary Shelley, and Jane Austen.* Chicago: University of Chicago Press, 1984.

Porter, Roy. *English Society in the Eighteenth Century.* Harmondsworth: Penguin Books, 1982.

Quinlan, Maurice J. *Victorian Prelude: A History of English Manners 1700–1830.* 1941; rpt. Hamden, Connecticut: Archon Books, 1965.

Radcliffe, Ann. *The Italian.* Ed. Frederick Garber. London: Oxford University Press, 1968.

―――. *The Mysteries of Udolpho*. Ed. Bonamy Dobrée. London: Oxford University Press, 1966.

―――. *The Romance of the Forest*. Ed. Chloe Chard. Oxford: Oxford University Press, 1986.

Roberts, Warren. *Jane Austen and the French Revolution*. London: Macmillan, 1979.

Rogers, Pat. 'Introduction'. *Pride and Prejudice*. Ed. Pat Rogers. Cambridge: Cambridge University Press, 2006.

Rosenfeld, Sybil. 'Jane Austen and Private Theatricals'. *Essays and Studies* 15 (1962), 40–51.

Sales, Roger. *Jane Austen and Representations of Regency England.* London: Routledge, 1994.

Shapard, David M., ed. *The Annotated Pride and Prejudice.* 2004; rpt. New York: Anchor Books, 2007.

Sleath, Eleanor. *The Orphan of the Rhine*. Ed. Devendra P. Varma. London: Folio Press, 1968.

Smith, LeRoy W. *Jane Austen and the Drama of Woman.* London: Macmillan, 1983.

Southam, B. C. 'General Tilney's Hot-houses: Some Recent Jane Austen Studies and Texts'. *Arid* 2 (1971), 52–62.

―――. *Jane Austen and the Navy*. 2nd ed. London: National Maritime Museum, 2005.

―――. '"Regulated Hatred" Revisited'. In *Jane Austen: 'Northanger Abbey' and 'Persuasion': A Casebook*. Ed. B. C. Southam. London: Macmillan, 1976, pp. 122–27.

―――. '*Sanditon*: The Seventh Novel'. In *Jane Austen's Achievement*. Ed. Juliet McMaster. London: Macmillan, 1976, pp. 1–26.

Southey, Robert. *Southey's Life of Nelson*. Ed. Geoffrey Callender. London: J. M. Dent, 1922.

Spacks, Patricia Meyer. 'Austen's Laughter'. *Women's Studies* 15 (1988), 71–85.

Spring, David. 'Interpreters of Jane Austen's Social World: Literary Critics and Historians'. In *Jane Austen: New Perspectives*. Ed. Janet Todd. New York: Holmes & Meier, 1983, pp. 53–72.

Stewart, Maaja A. *Domestic Realities and Imperial Fictions: Jane Austen's Novels in Eighteenth-Century Contexts.* Athens: University of Georgia Press, 1993.

Tanner, Tony. *Jane Austen.* London: Macmillan, 1986.

Thompson, E. P. *The Making of the English Working Class.* Harmondsworth: Penguin Books, 1980.

Tobin, Beth Fowkes. 'The Moral and Political Economy of Property in Austen's *Emma*'. In *Superintending the Poor: Charitable Ladies and Paternal Landlords in British Fiction, 1770–1860.* New Haven: Yale University Press, 1993, pp. 50–73.

Todd, Janet and Antje Blank. 'Introduction'. *Persuasion.* Ed. Janet Todd and Antie Blank. Cambridge: Cambridge University Press, 2006.

Tomalin, Claire. *Jane Austen: A Life.* New York: Alfred A. Knopf, 1997.

——. *The Life and Death of Mary Wollstonecraft.* London: Weidenfeld and Nicolson, 1974.

Trevelyan, G. M. *History of England.* Illustrated edition. 1926; rpt. London: Longman, 1973.

——. *English Social History: A Survey of Six Centuries, Chaucer to Queen Victoria.* 3rd ed. London: Longman, 1946.

Waldron, Mary. *Jane Austen and the Fiction of Her Time.* Cambridge: Cambridge University Press, 1999.

Wollstonecraft, Mary and William Godwin. *A Short Residence in Sweden, Norway and Denmark* and *Memoirs of the Author of The Rights of Woman.* Ed. Richard Holmes. Harmondsworth: Penguin Books, 1987.

Index

Association for the Preservation of Liberty and Property, 18–19
Auerbach, Erich, *Mimesis*, 31, 38–39
Auerbach, Nina, 'O Brave New World: Evolution and Revolution in *Persuasion*', 143 n.1
Austen, Charles, 123
Austen, Francis, 123–25, 131

Babb, Howard S, *Jane Austen's Novels: The Fabric of Dialogue*, 28, 37
Banfield, Ann, 'The Moral Landscape of *Mansfield Park*', 141 n. 2
Barnes, Donald Grove, *A History of the English Corn Laws from 1660 to 1846*, 146 n. 30
Bath, representation of, 89, 116–17
Bilger, Audrey, *Laughing Feminism: Subversive Comedy in Frances Burney, Maria Edgeworth, and Jane Austen*, 137 n. 2
Black, Eugene Charlton, *The Association: British Extraparliamentary Political Organization 1769–1793*, 134 n. 13
Blake, Robert, *The Conservative Party from Peel to Churchill*, 147 n. 31
Bristow, Edward J, *Vice and Vigilance: Purity Movements in Britain since 1700*, 138 n.6
Brown, Ford K, *Fathers of the Victorians: The Age of Wilberforce*, 138 n. 6
Brown, Julia Prewitt, *Jane Austen's Novels: Social Change and Literary Form*, 144 n. 2
Brummell, Beau, 84
Brunton, Mary, *Self-Control*, 83

Burke, Edmund, 61, 115–16; *Reflections on the Revolution in France*, 17
Burney, Fanny, 83
Butler, Marilyn, *Jane Austen and the War of Ideas*, 2

Cannan, Edwin. *A History of the Theories of Production and Distribution in English Political Economy from 1776 to 1848*, 126
Casal, Elvira, 'Laughing at Mr. Darcy: Wit and Sexuality in *Pride and Prejudice*', 137 n. 2
Chapman, R. W, 44, 57
Clarke, James Stanier, 146 n. 21
Coleridge, Samuel Taylor, *Biographia Literaria*, 19, 134 n. 16; *The Friend*, 19–20
Congreve, William, *The Way of the World*, 58
Copeland, Edward, *Women Writing about Money*, 24
Corn Laws, 127–28, 132
Cox, R. A, *Mansfield Park*, 78

Duckworth, Alistair M, *The Improvement of the Estate: A Study of Jane Austen's Novels*, 2, 14, 36, 94, 108, 137 n. 2, 140 n. 20, 144 n. 2
Duffy, Jr., Joseph M, 'Structure and Idea in Jane Austen's *Persuasion*', 144 n. 2

Enomoto, Minako, *Ōsuten no shōsetsu to sono shūhen* [The Novels of Jane Austen and Their Backgrounds], 25
Evangelicals, 6, 25–26, 55, 60, 72–73, 118; Jane Austen's comments on, 83, 141 n. 9

Fergus, Jan, *Jane Austen: A Literary Life*, 143 n. 12
Fielding, Henry, *Amelia*, 104; *The Covent-Garden Journal*, 59; *Joseph Andrews*, 59
French Revolution, 1, 6, 8, 10, 15–18, 55–56, 72
Fuseli, Henry, 42

Godwin, William, *Memoirs of the Author of The Rights of Woman*, 41, 43

Harris, Jocelyn, *A Revolution Almost beyond Expression: Jane Austen's* Persuasion, 124, 146 n. 22

Hemlow, Joyce, 'Fanny Burney and the Courtesy Books', 141 n. 8
Hodge, Jane Aiken, *The Double Life of Jane Austen*, 26
Hole, Robert, 139 n. 14
Hopkins, Robert, 'General Tilney and Affairs of State: The Political Gothic of *Northanger Abbey*', 19–20
Hubback, J. H. and Edith C, *Jane Austen's Sailor Brothers*, 123, 125

Imlay, Gilbert, 42–43

Jaeger, Muriel, *Before Victoria: Changing Standards and Behaviour 1787–1837*, 67–68, 80
Johnson, Claudia L, *Jane Austen: Women, Politics, and the Novel*, 2, 40–41, 93, 147 n. 36

Kent, Christopher, '"Real Solemn History" and Social History', 25
Kliger, Samuel, 'Jane Austen's *Pride and Prejudice* in the Eighteenth-Century Mode', 60–61
Kramp, Michael, *Disciplining Love: Austen and the Modern Man*, 138 n. 7

Lamb, Caroline, 57
Lamb, Charles, 138 n. 4
Lane, Maggie, *A Charming Place: Bath in the Life and Times of Jane Austen*, 144 n. 8
Lavery, Brian, *Nelson's Navy: The Ships, Men and Organisation 1793–1815*, 121–22
Letters, Jane Austen's, 44, 49, 83, 124, 141 n. 9
Lewis, Michael, *A Social History of the Navy 1793–1815*, 120–21, 145 nn. 13, 14
Lincoln, Abraham, 56
Litz, A. Walton, *Jane Austen: A Study of Her Artistic Development*, 61
Lodge, David, 'The Vocabulary of *Mansfield Park*', 80

MacDonagh, Oliver, *Jane Austen: Real and Imagined Worlds*, 97, 101
Malcolmson, Robert W, *Popular Recreations in English Society 1700–1850*, 142 n. 11
Marshall, John, *Royal Naval Biography*, 68, 145 n. 13

Mingay, G. E, *English Landed Society in the Eighteenth Century*, 65–66; *The Gentry: The Rise and Fall of a Ruling Class*, 9, 113–14, 142 n. 8

Mitford, Mary Russell, 63, 67

Modert, Jo, 'Chronology within the Novels', 147 n. 32

Moler, Kenneth L, *Jane Austen's Art of Allusion*, 129; *Pride and Prejudice: A Study in Artistic Economy*, 61

Molière, *Le Misanthrope*, 31, 38–39

Monaghan, David, *Jane Austen: Structure and Social Vision*, 115, 144 nn. 2, 6

Moody, Ellen, 'A Calendar for *Persuasion*', 147 n. 32

More, Hannah, comment on the society in the 1810s, 68; *Cheap Repository Tracts*, 55; *Cœlebs in Search of a Wife*, 25, 83; *Strictures on the Modern System of Female Education*, 60; *Thoughts on the Importance of the Manners of the Great to General Society*, 83

Napoleonic wars, 1, 126

Nardin, Jane. 'Charity in *Emma*', 103, 107, 143 n. 15; *Those Elegant Decorum: The Concept of Propriety in Jane Austen's Novels*, 79, 98, 100, 136 n. 6, 138 n. 5, 140 nn. 20, 21, 142 n. 6

Nelson, Horatio, 121, 124–26

O'Byrne, William, *A Naval Biographical Dictionary*, 68, 145 n. 13

Parker, Keiko, '"What Part of Bath Do You Think They Will Settle In?": Jane Austen's Use of Bath in *Persuasion*', 116–17

Parker, Mark, 'The End of Emma: Drawing the Boundaries of Class in Austen', 109

Paulson, Ronald, *Representations of Revolution (1789–1820)*, 16–17

Perkin, Harold, *The Origins of Modern English Society 1780–1880*, 9, 131, 142 n. 3, 147 nn. 37, 38

Poovey, Mary, *The Proper Lady and the Woman Writer: Ideology as Style in the Works of Mary Wollstonecraft, Mary Shelley, and Jane Austen*, 40, 46

Porter, Roy, *English Society in the Eighteenth Century*, 142 n. 3

Quinlan, Maurice J, *Victorian Prelude: A History of English Manners 1700–1830*, 138 n. 6

Radcliffe, Ann. *The Italian*, 17–18; *The Mysteries of Udolpho*, 16; *The Romance of the Forest*, 17
Roberts, Warren, *Jane Austen and the French Revolution*, 19
Rogers, Pat, 139 n. 9
Rosenfeld, Sybil, 'Jane Austen and Private Theatricals', 141 n. 10

Sales, Roger, *Jane Austen and Representations of Regency England*, 119
Shapard, David M, *The Annotated Pride and Prejudice*, 50, 138 n. 8
Sleath, Eleanor, *The Orphan of the Rhine*, 17
Smith, LeRoy W, *Jane Austen and the Drama of Woman*, 40
Southam, B. C., 'General Tilney's Hot-houses; Some Recent Jane Austen Studies and Texts', 22; *Jane Austen and the Navy*, 123, 145 n. 19; '"Regulated Hatred" Revisited', 15–16, 19; '*Sanditon*: The Seventh Novel', 135 nn. 26, 26, 142 n. 12
Southey, Robert, *Life of Nelson*, 124–26
Spacks, Patricia Meyer, 'Austen's Laughter', 137 n. 2
Spring, David, 'Interpreters of Jane Austen's Social World: Literary Critics and Historians', 22–23, 106, 112
Stewart, Maaja A, *Domestic Realities and Imperial Fictions: Jane Austen's Novels in Eighteenth-Century Contexts*, 139 n. 10

Tanner, Tony, *Jane Austen*, 24, 33, 111–12, 138 n. 5, 141 n. 2, 142 n. 2
Thompson, E. P., *The Making of the English Working Class*, 19
Tobin, Beth Fowkes, 'The Moral and Political Economy of Property in Austen's *Emma*', 107
Todd, Janet and Antje Blank, 145 n. 11, 147 n. 33
Tomalin, Claire, *Jane Austen: A Life*, 106; *The Life and Death of Mary Wollstonecraft*, 43–44, 137 n. 22
Trevelyan, G. M., *History of England*, 1; *English Social History: A Survey of Six Centuries, Chaucer to Queen Victoria*, 146 n. 29

Waldron, Mary, *Jane Austen and the Fiction of Her Time*, 147 n. 35
Wollstonecraft, Mary, 41–47; *A Short Residence in Sweden, Norway and Denmark*, 41–42

著者紹介
三馬志伸（みんま　しのぶ）

1959年千葉県生まれ。
慶應義塾大学大学院博士課程単位取得満期退学。
現在、玉川大学文学部教授。

JANE AUSTEN IN AND OUT OF CONTEXT

2012年9月29日　初版第1刷発行

著　者───三馬志伸
発行者───坂上　弘
発行所───慶應義塾大学出版会株式会社
　　　　　〒108-8346　東京都港区三田2-19-30
　　　　　TEL　〔編集部〕03-3451-0931
　　　　　　　　〔営業部〕03-3451-3584〈ご注文〉
　　　　　　　　〔　〃　〕03-3451-6926
　　　　　FAX　〔営業部〕03-3451-3122
　　　　　振替　00190-8-155497
　　　　　URL http://www.keio-up.co.jp/
装　丁───土屋　光（Perfect Vacuum）
組　版───ステラ
印刷・製本──中央精版印刷株式会社

©2012 Shinobu Minma
Printed in Japan　ISBN 978-4-7664-1961-0